Who was shooting at her and why?

None of this made any sense, but there was no mistaking that those bullets had been meant for her. Her heart pounded so loudly in her ears she couldn't hear anything else. Why was this happening? What was going on? The sight of Jake barreling out of the front door with a gun in his hand forced a sob of relief to escape her lips.

He fired several shots into the woods where the original bullets had come from as he ran toward her.

"You all right?" he asked, his voice a terse snap of tension.

She gave a curt nod, unable to find her voice.

"Did you see anyone?" he asked.

"No, I just felt the first bullet buzz by my head and I ran." A tremble tried to take hold of her body but she fought against it, knowing she couldn't give in to her fear until she was safe and sound.

She certainly felt safer with Jake by her side, but someplace out there was somebody who had apparently just tried to kill her not once, not twice, but three times.

Dear Reader,

I love babies. I love their smell, their drooling smiles and their cuddly warmth. If my husband would have agreed I would have filled our house with babies, and then given each of them away when they got to be teenagers!

When Grace Sinclair gets pregnant after a crazy one night stand, she's horrified to find herself carrying not one baby, not twins, but triplets and with the daddy of the babies only a distant memory in her mind.

With the help of MysteryMom, a cyber friend, she finally locates the daddy working the family ranch with his brothers. But, when Grace goes to the ranch for a family reunion, she's in for a surprise. Not only does danger come her way, but also so does an unexpected love.

All she has to do is survive a cunning killer and keep her babies safe to get the happily-ever-after she and her daughters deserve.

Enjoy and keep reading!

Carla Cassidy

Cowboy's Triplet Trouble

CARLA CASSIDY.

MILLS & BOON®

First published in Great Britain 2012
by Mills & Boon, an imprint of Harlequin (UK) Limited.
Large Print edition 2012
Harlequin (UK) Limited,
Eton House, 18-24 Paradise Road,
Richmond, Surrey TW9 1SR

LP

© Carla Bracale 2011

ISBN: 978 0 263 22997 4

Harlequin (UK) policy is to use papers that are natural, renewable and recyclable products and made from wood grown in sustainable forests. The logging and manufacturing process conform to the legal environmental regulations of the country of origin.

Printed and bound in Great Britain
by CPI Antony Rowe, Chippenham, Wiltshire

CARLA CASSIDY

is an award-winning author who has written over eighty books for Mills & Boon. In 1995, she won Best Silhouette Romance from *RT Book Reviews* for *Anything for Danny*. In 1998, she also won a Career Achievement Award for Best Innovative Series from *RT Book Reviews*.

Carla believes the only thing better than curling up with a good book to read is sitting down at the computer with a good story to write. She's looking forward to writing many more books and bringing hours of pleasure to readers.

To Gretchen Jones,
My personal computer genius,
back deck sitter and shoe fetish friend.
Thanks for your friendship
and support. I appreciate you!

Chapter 1

"I can't believe you're going to do something so risky," Natalie Sinclair exclaimed.

Grace leaned back in the kitchen chair and smiled at her younger sister. "This conversation is backward. Isn't it usually me saying stuff like that to you?"

The two were seated in Grace's kitchen where the late May afternoon breeze drifted through the open windows, bringing with it the sweet scents of early summer.

"That's because normally I'm the one doing

the crazy, reckless things," Natalie replied. She picked up her lemonade and took a sip, eyeing Grace over the top of the glass as if suspecting her older sister had been replaced by a look-alike alien. "Maybe this is some sort of postpartum insanity," she said as she placed her glass back on the table.

Grace laughed. "It's been almost a year since I was pregnant. This definitely isn't postpartum anything." Her laughter faded as she leaned forward. "I have to do this, Natalie. I've made up my mind, and I'm leaving first thing in the morning."

Natalie shook her head. "At least give me the directions to where you'll be so I know where to send the police when you're in trouble."

Grace opened the manila folder next to her laptop and took out a piece of paper. "I already intended to give you the details, although I'm certainly not expecting any trouble." She handed Natalie the directions she'd printed off her computer earlier in the morning.

"You're leaving here to travel almost two hundred miles away to a place you've never been before because some person on the internet, who you've never met, told you to go there. Gee, sounds brilliant to me," Natalie said sarcastically.

Grace felt an uncharacteristic flush heat her cheeks. "It's not just anyone. It's Mystery-Mom."

"Yeah, and for all you know this Mystery-Mom is some fifty-year-old male pervert sitting around in his underwear and talking to you over the computer."

Once again Grace couldn't help but laugh.

"I've been corresponding through email with MysteryMom for almost two years now. I'd think if that were the case I would have gotten a clue by now. Besides, I'm taking my gun with me."

Both Grace and Natalie had gotten handguns from their mother on their twenty-first birthdays, unusual gifts from a strong, nontraditional woman. She had endured a violent mugging and had sworn her daughters would never be helpless victims.

"At least that makes me feel a little better," Natalie conceded.

"It would make me feel a little better if you had a job. Are you putting in applications everywhere?" Grace asked, eager to get the conversation off her plans and on to something else. Certainly Natalie's lack of employment was a concern, especially since she wasn't going to school either. She was twenty-four years old and just seemed to be drifting through her life at the moment.

"Sure, I'm trying, but I can't find anyone who wants to hire me."

"Maybe if you'd take that ring out of your eyebrow somebody would be more interested in giving you a job," Grace replied gently. "Or you could go back to school and get some training. You have the money to do that and you could decide to go into whatever field you wanted to."

"Okay, that's my clue to get out of here," Natalie said, not hiding her irritation. She checked her watch. "Not only do I not want one of your loving lectures, but I'm meeting Jimmy in a few minutes for a late lunch."

"When do I get to meet this paragon of

virtue that you've been dating?" Grace asked as they both rose from the table.

Natalie gave her a secretive little smile. "When I'm good and ready for you to meet him." Together the two walked to the front door. "You'll call me as soon as you get to where you're going tomorrow and let me know that you're okay?"

"Of course I will," Grace replied and pulled Natalie close for a quick hug. There was almost ten years' difference in their ages, and Grace had always mothered Natalie. Now that their mother was gone, she felt especially maternal toward her younger sister.

Natalie stepped out of the embrace and opened the front door. "You know the routine. You've said it often enough to me. Drive carefully and be aware of any potential trouble around you."

"I will. And when I get home I want to meet this Jimmy of yours," Grace replied.

Natalie waved her hand as she headed toward her expensive little sports car in the driveway.

Grace watched until Natalie's car zoomed out of sight and then shut the door and walked back into the living room.

For a moment she simply stood in the middle of the room and listened to the silence. It was rare for the house to be so quiet. Grace hoped it would stay that way for another thirty minutes or more so that she could finish packing for her road trip in the morning.

She scooted into her bedroom, determined to take advantage of what little time she had. As she began to pack the open suitcase on the bed, she tried not to think about what Natalie had said, but her words kept echoing in Grace's head.

Risky? Grace had only done one risky thing in her entire life and the consequence of that particular action had changed her life forever.

No, she didn't believe what she planned for the next day was particularly risky. As crazy as it sounded, she trusted the woman who had been her cyberfriend for almost two years. MysteryMom had been a source of support and comfort from the time Grace had found herself pregnant until now. She had never given Grace a reason not to trust her.

Grace put the last blouse in the suitcase and then closed and latched it. She left her bedroom and went to the doorway of the room next to hers.

The walls were a powder-pink and the furniture was white. There was a double dresser, a rocking chair and three cribs, each one holding a precious ten-month-old.

Grace leaned against the doorjamb as her thoughts drifted back in time, back to the night she'd attended her best friend's wedding.

The wedding had been glorious and the reception had been a wild party. The handsome cowboy from Oklahoma had danced and flirted with her as they'd downed glasses of champagne like water throughout the entire event.

When she'd awakened the next morning in her hotel room bed with him next to her, she'd been horrified. She'd stumbled out of the bed and into the bathroom. The hangover she'd suffered was nothing compared to the embarrassment that flooded through her as she realized what she had done…what they had done.

When she'd left the bathroom he was gone, and she'd shoved her first and only one-night stand to the back of her mind. She'd returned to her life as a third-grade schoolteacher and hadn't thought about him again. Until two months later when she'd discovered she was pregnant.

It was at that time that she'd tried to find him. But she only knew he was from some-place in Oklahoma and she thought his name had been Justin. She'd called her friend who had gotten married that night, but Sally had told her that the cowboy had been a friend of a friend and she had no idea what his last name was or exactly where he was from.

Two months after that, when the doctor told Grace she was expecting triplets, she'd stopped trying to find the father and instead had focused all her energy on preparing herself to be the mother of three babies.

It wasn't until a week ago that MysteryMom had sent her a message indicating that she thought she'd found the cowboy. His name was Justin Johnson and he operated a ranch with his brothers just outside of Tulsa, Oklahoma.

Grace had no idea how her cyberfriend had come up with the information, but it felt right. She vaguely remembered Justin telling her he ranched with a couple of brothers.

She'd sat on the information for several days and then yesterday morning, after a slightly traumatic event the night before, had decided to pack up the girls and drive to his ranch outside the small town of Cameron Creek, Oklahoma.

She now smiled as Abby peeked over the

crib railing. Her dark curls were tousled from her nap and a delighted smile curved her rosebud lips.

Grace hurried over and picked her up, hoping to sneak her out of the room before she awakened her sisters. But at that moment Bonnie and Casey also woke up, squealing to get down and breaking the silence that had momentarily gripped the house.

It was after nine the next morning when the girls were finally loaded in their car seats and Grace left her house, heading to a ranch just over the Kansas state line in Oklahoma.

Thankfully it was Saturday and the Wichita traffic was light, making getting out of town a breeze. But she wouldn't have needed to worry about traffic for a while. Summer vacation had begun a week earlier, and she had almost three months to do whatever she wanted and spend time with the daughters who were her heart.

She loved teaching, and it was wonderful to be working at a job that gave her summers off, especially now that she was a mommy of three.

The girls were contented passengers, especially since Grace had armed them with their favorite toys, oat cereal in plastic snack containers and sippy cups filled with apple juice. They chattered and giggled for the first hour of the trip and then eventually fell asleep, leaving Grace with only the softly playing radio music and her own thoughts.

MysteryMom. She'd met the woman in a chat room for single mothers when she'd first discovered she was pregnant, and the friendship had been instantaneous. It had been MysteryMom who had helped Grace cope with morning sickness and swollen feet, who had talked her through the fears of raising triplets all alone.

When Grace's mother had fallen down a staircase and died when the babies had been only a month old, it had been MysteryMom that Grace had turned to for comfort.

Even after MysteryMom had given her the information about Justin Johnson, Grace hadn't been sure she wanted to make contact. But then a near-fatal car accident had made up her mind. That night she'd realized that if something happened to her there was nobody to take care of the girls except Natalie—who shouldn't have care of a goldfish.

She now glanced at the directions Mystery-Mom had given her to the Rockin' J Ranch. She couldn't imagine that MysteryMom had any ulterior motive other than to help Grace find the man who had fathered her triplets.

Grace wanted nothing from the handsome cowboy who had shared her bed for a single night after too much alcohol. She certainly didn't expect any kind of a relationship with a man who had never tried to contact her again after that night.

But she did believe he had a right to know that he was a father, and she hoped that he would want to be a part of the girls' lives.

She wanted that. She wanted that more than anything for her daughters. She'd never had a father in her life, and the old saying that you can't miss what you never had simply wasn't true. The absence of a father had resonated deeply. Not only in Grace's soul, but, she suspected, in Natalie's heart and soul as well. Of course, she couldn't imagine any man taking a look at the sweet baby faces of her daughters and not wanting to be a part of their lives.

Thankfully, the small town of Cameron Creek, Oklahoma, had a motel, and she'd already booked a room for the night with the understanding that she might stay longer. If MysteryMom was right and Justin was at the address Grace had been given, then Grace was prepared to stay a couple of days in the motel so he could spend some time with the girls and they could decide how to handle things in the future.

She slowed the car as she realized she was near the turnoff that would lead to the Rockin' J Ranch. She was vaguely surprised the sleeping babies in the backseat couldn't hear the thump of her heartbeat.

Nerves. She was suddenly incredibly nervous. Afraid that she'd been a fool to trust a woman she'd never met in person before. Afraid that this was all some crazy wild-goose chase.

Patting her purse, she felt herself calm somewhat. Her gun was inside, loaded and ready to use if necessary. She wouldn't hesitate to fire it if she sensed her own safety or, more importantly, her children's safety was in peril.

Her nerves eased a little more as she reached the entrance to the ranch. Massive stones with wooden plaques indicated it was the ranch she sought. In the distance a two-story house rose out of the lush pastures. The ranch looked huge and well-kept, definitely not the place you'd expect an old man to be sitting around in his underwear and pretending to be a woman named MysteryMom.

Still, as she pulled up in front of the house

and parked the car, the first thing she did was pull her gun out of her purse and slip it into the pocket of her navy blazer.

"Better safe than sorry," she muttered beneath her breath. The girls were still soundly sleeping as she got out of the car. She'd left her car window cracked open a bit to allow in the sweet summer breeze, and she figured it would only take a minute to find out if she was at the right place or not.

Her nerves twisted in her stomach as she walked toward the front door. The worst that could happen was this would be the wrong place, the wrong man, and if that was the case then she and the girls would check into their motel room and make the trek back home in the morning.

It was just before noon, and she didn't see anyone around. A large barn stood not too far in the distance, along with several other outbuildings. Maybe everyone had knocked off work for the lunch hour or were out in the pasture where she couldn't see them.

As she reached the porch, she gave one last look at the car and reminded herself that she was doing this for the little girls asleep there. With one hand on the butt of the gun in her pocket, she used the other hand to knock on the door.

When the door opened, Grace's breath caught in the back of her throat. She stared at the man who was the father of her daughters.

She'd forgotten just how hot he was with his curly black hair and chiseled features. The last time she'd seen him he'd been wearing a dark suit and white dress shirt. He now wore a pair of tight, faded blue jeans that showcased his slim hips and a white T-shirt that stretched across his broad shoulders.

A coil of heat began to unfurl in the pit of her stomach. It stopped as she saw the utter blankness in his dark blue eyes. Instead of the heat, a cold wind of embarrassment blew through her. He didn't even remember her.

"Yes?" he asked with the pleasant smile of somebody greeting a stranger.

She was struck by a new attack of nerves. "Wait here," she said and turned and left the large porch. She hurried toward the car, her heart pounding a million miles a minute.

She was a third-grade teacher. Maybe the best way to let him know what had happened since the last time she'd seen him was a little show-and-tell. She opened the trunk with the press of a button on her key chain and quickly withdrew the oversize stroller.

It took her only moments to unfold the stroller and fill the seats with sleeping little girls and a diaper bag. As she pushed the girls toward the house, she saw his expression transform from pleasant to utterly stunned.

"Let me jog your memory," she said when she reached the porch again. "Nineteen months ago, Sally and David's wedding? My name is Grace…Grace Sinclair. We were together at the wedding and the next morning you left me with a surprise. I'd like you to meet your daughters."

"Maybe you should come inside where we can talk," he said, his eyes dark and troubled. "I'm afraid you've made a mistake. I'm not the man you're looking for. I've never seen you before in my life."

Jake Johnson instantly knew he'd said the wrong thing. Her pretty cheeks filled with color as her green eyes narrowed dangerously. "The last thing I expected from you was a denial of even meeting me," she replied, her voice icy with an edge of contempt. "Surely you remember being at the wedding."

"Please, come inside where we can talk more comfortably." Jake grabbed one end of the stroller to pull it up the stairs and into the house. As he gazed at the sleeping girls, there was no doubt in his mind that they were Johnsons. Their little heads were covered with dark curly hair and the shape of their faces reminded him of baby photos he'd seen of himself.

And there was no doubt in his mind of exactly who was responsible for this woman being on his porch with three babies. His stomach knotted with a touch of anger. This was one mess that wasn't going to just go away. Jake wouldn't be able to pay a ticket, take care of a fine or do some fast talking to make this one disappear.

Once they had the stroller inside the living room, he gestured her to the sofa. As she lowered herself down, he sat in the overstuffed chair opposite her.

He couldn't help but notice that Grace Sinclair was a gorgeous woman. Her long brown hair held shiny blond highlights, and her legs seemed to go on forever beneath the navy slacks she wore. At the moment her beautiful green eyes were filled with anger, and her lush lips were compressed tightly together as she glared at him.

"I didn't exactly think you'd jump for joy at the unexpected news that you were a father, especially a father of three," she said. "I know it was only one night, but we were together for a long time at the reception."

"I should explain that…." he began.

"Of course, maybe you make it a habit of sleeping with lots of women and don't always remember them when you meet them again out of a bed," she continued, cutting him off midsentence. "Allow me to remind you again—Sally's wedding in Wichita?"

"I wasn't—"

"Look, if you're worried that I want something from you, that I might need anything from you, then don't. I just thought you had a right to know that you are a father."

"I'm not saying that—"

"I'll gladly have a DNA test done if that's what you want." She sat up straighter on the sofa and tucked a strand of her shiny hair behind her ear. "I know for sure that you're the father because I hadn't been with anyone for a long time before you and I wasn't with anyone after you. But I would understand if you have doubts considering the circumstances."

Once again her cheeks became a charming shade of red. "You don't really know me. You don't know what kind of a woman I am, and I can understand how the fact that I fell into bed with you so easily that night might make you think I do that all the time—which couldn't be further from the truth. I've never done anything like that before. My only excuse is that night for the first time in my life, I drank too much."

Jake didn't even try to say anything. He sensed she wasn't finished yet, and in any case wouldn't let him get a word in edgewise. The anger he'd felt moments before had passed, and instead a weary resignation had set in.

It was obvious what had happened—a wedding party, a night of too much booze and unprotected sex. Now somebody was going to have to step up and do the right thing. Jake knew for certain it wasn't going to be him.

Sometimes he felt as if he'd spent every day of his thirty-five years doing what was right for everyone else. Now it was his turn to do what was right for him, and there was no way he intended to get caught up in this drama.

Yet, even as he thought it, he knew there was no way he wouldn't be sucked into the mess. The precious little girls asleep in the stroller would ensure that he became a part of it in some way.

"I don't need any child support from you. I

just thought you might want to be a dad to the girls. Girls need fathers in their lives."

There was a wealth of emotion in her voice, then she finally took a breath and stared at him expectantly. At that moment Jake's brother appeared in the doorway between the living room and the kitchen.

Grace's mouth formed a perfect O as she looked from one man to the other. Just then one of the little girls woke up with a cry, as if protesting the fact that her mother had no idea when it came to the question of who was the daddy.

Chapter 2

Grace looked from one man to the other, astonished as she realized they were obviously identical twins. No wonder the man seated across from her had insisted he didn't know her. He *didn't* know her.

She dug Abby's sippy cup out of the diaper bag and handed it to her, an action that immediately stopped Abby's tears and brought a happy smile to her face. Twins, for crying out loud. How was she supposed to know that the man she'd slept with had a twin?

At that moment a woman appeared behind the man in the doorway. She was a plump, pretty blonde. She placed a hand on his shoulder. "Honey, what's going on?" she asked. She took one look at the stroller and clapped her hands together. "Oh my goodness, aren't they precious?"

Grace's heart sank to the ground. If the man seated on the chair opposite her wasn't the girls' father, then the man in the doorway must be. A look at his hand showed her he was wearing a gold wedding ring that matched the one on the woman's finger.

Married. Oh, God, had he been married on the night they'd slept together? Had he ditched his wedding band for a quick fling while out of town? The very idea horrified her. The last thing Grace would ever do was get involved in any way with a married man.

"I think maybe introductions are in order," the man in the chair said. "I'm Jake Johnson, and that's my brother Jeffrey and his wife, Kerri."

"I'm so sorry. I've obviously made some sort of mistake," Grace said as she rose to her feet. Jeffrey…Justin…maybe she'd gotten his name wrong at the wedding. Certainly coming here had been a terrible mistake.

She didn't want to screw up a marriage. This had suddenly become an awful nightmare and all she wanted to do was escape from it all. "I'll just take the girls and we'll be on our way."

"Grace—may I call you Grace?" Jake asked. She nodded and he motioned her back to the sofa. "Please sit down. Jeffrey isn't the father of your daughters either."

"Heavens, no!" Jeffrey replied. "I'd eventually like to have children, but I definitely want to do that with my wife." He looped an arm around Kerri's shoulder and smiled at her lovingly.

"I think you're looking for our brother," Jake said.

"There's more of you?" Grace felt as if she'd entered either a comedy of errors or the Twilight Zone.

Jake gave her a tight smile. "One more. Justin. We're triplets."

Grace breathed a sigh of relief, although she was more than a little embarrassed that she'd just given Jake Johnson far more personal information than she'd ever want him to know. "Is Justin here?"

"He isn't," Jake replied.

"But he almost always shows up around dinnertime," Kerri said as she approached the stroller. "May I?" She gestured to Abby, who raised her hands to get out of her confinement.

Grace nodded and checked her wristwatch. It was just after noon. "Could you contact Justin and see if maybe he could come by earlier? Otherwise I'll just take the girls to the motel room where I'd planned to stay for the night and he can contact me there."

"Nonsense," Kerri said briskly. "I've got lunch ready and of course you and the girls will stay and eat with us." She laughed as Abby grabbed her nose with a giggle.

"I don't want to impose," Grace protested. The whole thing felt awkward. At that moment the other two girls woke up and suddenly chaos reigned.

"We definitely need introductions to these

sweet girls," Kerri said as her husband pulled Bonnie from the stroller and Grace got Casey.

"You have Abby, Jeffrey has Bonnie and I have Casey," Grace said. Each of the girls grinned as they heard their names. "And as you can see, they haven't met anyone they don't like yet. Although Casey here is definitely the most shy." She frowned. "Maybe it would be best if I just go to the motel and you can tell Justin to meet me there."

"You're here now," Jake said rather curtly. "You might as well stay for lunch and I'll see if I can get Justin on his cell phone." As he left the room Grace felt some of the tension that had coiled in her belly ease. At least Jeffrey hadn't been in the room when she'd told Jake that she'd been nothing more than a drunken one-night stand with Justin. Gosh, how utterly embarrassing.

"Jeffrey, why don't you go out to the shed and bring in the old high chairs," Kerri said, obviously a woman accustomed to being in command. "And while you do that, Grace and I will go into the kitchen and get to know each other a little better."

"Sounds like a plan," Jeffrey replied agreeably. He set Bonnie on her bottom at his feet and headed toward the door.

Grace felt as if everything was quickly spinning out of control and she didn't quite know how to get any control back. At that moment Jake returned to the room. "Justin didn't answer, but I left him a message to come here as soon as he can," he said.

"We were just about to take the girls into the kitchen," Kerri said. "But we seem to be short one pair of hands."

"The story of my life," Grace muttered beneath her breath.

Jake bent down and picked up Bonnie. He carried her away from his body, as if he'd never carried a baby before and wasn't sure he liked it. At that moment Grace decided she wasn't at all sure she liked him very much.

The kitchen was enormous, filled with sunshine from the floor-to-ceiling windows that created one wall. A heavy wooden table big enough to comfortably seat eight held place settings for three and a steaming casserole dish that smelled of chicken.

"Let's put the girls here on the floor," Kerri said. "I'll get them some plastic containers to occupy them while I finish getting lunch on the table and you and I can have a nice chat." She smiled at Grace, a friendly gesture that took some of the sharp edge off Grace's tension.

At least Natalie had been wrong about the person living here being a fifty-year-old pervert. "Where did Jeffrey go?" Jake asked as he gingerly set Bonnie on the red-and-white throw rug on the floor.

"I told him to see about the old high chairs in the shed," Kerri replied.

"I'll go see if he needs help." He escaped out the back door, taking with him much of the energy in the room.

Within minutes the girls were all on the rug with a variety of plastic spoons, bowls and lids to keep them happy. Grace sat at the table while Kerri bustled around the kitchen to finish preparing the meal and laid another place setting.

"How on earth do you tell them apart?"

Kerri asked as she placed bread and butter on the table.

"Even though at first glance they look identical, there are subtle differences. Bonnie wrinkles her nose when she laughs and Casey's hair is just a shade lighter. To make it easier on everyone else, I just dress them in different colors. Abby is pink, Bonnie is blue and Casey is yellow."

"It's the same with Jake, Jeffrey and Justin," Kerri said. "Most people insist they can't tell them apart, but there are definite differences. Jake is definitely the alpha dog and his eyes are slightly darker than his brothers. My Jeffrey is thinner than the other two and sweeter tempered." Her voice held a wealth of love. "And you know Justin."

That was the whole problem. Grace didn't *know* Justin at all. She was ashamed to admit that she barely remembered being intimate with him. What she did remember from that night was how good the champagne had tasted and how Justin made sure her glass remained full and his flirting attention remained solely on her. "Do you all live here?" she asked.

Kerri placed a large salad on the table and then eased down in the chair next to Grace. "This was the family homestead but their parents died twelve years ago when they were all twenty-two. Jake took over running the ranch."

She laughed. "But that's not what you asked. To answer your question, Justin lives in an apartment in Cameron Creek and Jeffrey and I are only living here for another couple of weeks or so. We have a house being built on the property. And once we get moved in I want one of those." She pointed to the girls, who were gibbering and playing, perfectly content at the moment.

"Be careful what you wish for," Grace said with a smile. "I always wanted a son or a daughter. Apparently that triplet gene is strong, and despite how well they're doing now, they don't always stay all in the same place."

At that moment Jeffrey and Jake returned, carrying high chairs that looked as if they were from another era. "They're old," Jeffrey said, "but we cleaned them up and they will still serve their purpose. Thank goodness that old shed hasn't been cleaned out in years."

"Perfect timing," Kerri said as she jumped up from the table.

She helped Grace get the girls settled in the high chairs and then they all sat down to eat.

The little girls had bowls with a bit of the casserole and green beans. Grace had retrieved their cups from the diaper bag and they dug into their meal with their usual enthusiasm.

"You didn't mention where you're from," Jake said as he passed her the bowl of green beans.

There was something about the directness of his gaze that she found more than a bit unsettling. Kerri was right. Now that Grace had spent a little time with him she couldn't imagine how she'd initially thought he was the man who had fathered her girls.

The cowboy she'd met at the wedding had been fun and flirty, with a bit of wildness in his blue eyes. Jake looked harder, his eyes a midnight-blue. He definitely looked as if he'd never lose control enough to drink too much, let alone wind up in a bed with a woman he barely knew.

"Wichita," she replied.

"Nice place," Jeffrey said as he buttered a slice of bread. "What do you do there?"

"I'm a third-grade teacher."

Grace was grateful when the conversation changed from her to the ranch and the work being completed on Jeffrey and Kerri's house. As the meal and talk progressed it became evident to Grace that Bonnie was flirting with Jake.

Her high chair was next to his chair at the table, and she fluttered her long, thick eyelashes as she cast him one toothy grin after another. He didn't pay attention until she managed to grab his arm, grin and offer him a slightly smooshed green bean.

Kerri laughed. "Looks as though you have a little admirer, Jake."

He eyed the green bean as if it was something he'd never seen before in his life and was highly suspicious of where it might have come from. Bonnie gibbered to him and pressed the bean closer.

"Uh…thanks," he said as he finally took the bean from her and placed it gingerly on the edge of his plate.

Bonnie clapped her hands together in happiness, her button nose wrinkling as she smiled, then fluttered her eyes, making her long dark lashes dance.

Jake focused back on his plate and Grace was thankful he wasn't the father. He obviously had no interest in children and didn't appear to have any softness inside him. She definitely wanted more than somebody like him to be a part of her girls' lives.

She wanted a man who would be unable to resist the flutter of Bonnie's lashes, the sweetness of Casey's smiles and Abby's infectious giggles. She wanted a man who would be unable to resist loving them with all his heart.

The food was good and the conversation was light and easy with Kerri filling most of the awkward silences with friendly chatter. Still, Grace decided if Justin hadn't shown up by the time lunch was over and she helped with the cleanup, she'd go on to the motel and get settled in there for the night.

She'd intruded enough on these people. Granted they were Abby, Bonnie and Casey's aunt and uncles, but there was no way to know what part they'd play in each other's lives until she spoke to Justin.

In the best of worlds, no matter what happened with Justin, these people would want to stay involved with the little girls. But Grace was realistic enough to know that life didn't always work that way. In fact, in her experience life rarely worked out the way it was supposed to.

The meal was just about finished when Grace's cell phone rang. It was in the opposite pocket from the gun in her blazer. She recognized the number of the caller and excused herself from the table.

"Natalie," she said as she answered. "I'm so sorry. I forgot to call when I got here."

"So, what's happening? Are you at the right place? Is he wearing a dirty undershirt and tighty whities?"

Grace laughed. "Yes and no. Yes, I'm at the right place, but I'm still waiting to meet with

Justin." She quickly explained about the men being triplets and that she was waiting for the father of the girls to show up at the house. Promising to stay in touch, she ended the call and hurried back into the kitchen.

"I'm so sorry," she said to the others still seated at the table. "That was my younger sister. I'd promised to call her the minute I arrived here and then promptly forgot to do so. She was worried."

"You only have the one sister?" Kerri asked.

Grace sat back down in her chair. "Thankfully yes," she said with a touch of humor. "Natalie is twenty-four, almost ten years younger than me, and some days it feels like I have four children instead of three."

"What about your parents?" Jeffrey asked.

"We were raised by a single mother and she passed away nine months ago," Grace replied.

She was acutely aware of Jake's gaze on her. Dark and unreadable, the intensity made her slightly uncomfortable.

"Jake, what's up?" A familiar deep male voice called from the living room.

Grace's stomach clenched tight as she realized Justin had arrived. Certainly the friendliness toward her and the children by the people around the table had given her hope, and that hope now surged up inside her.

She wasn't expecting instant happiness from Justin, but what she was hoping for was some sort of acceptance of the situation and the happiness would come later.

He came into the kitchen. In that first instant of seeing Justin again, Grace couldn't imagine how she'd mistaken Jake for him. Justin looked younger and his hair was longer and slightly wild with curls.

His blue eyes widened at the sight of her, and then he looked at the three girls in the high chairs. "Oh, hell no!" he exclaimed and then turned and ran out of the kitchen.

Jake watched Grace's lovely face pale as she jumped up from her chair. "Please excuse me," she said, her voice trembling as she left the kitchen, obviously in pursuit of Justin.

There was a long moment of silence around the table.

"Mama?" Bonnie said, but didn't seem upset by Grace's absence.

"She seems really nice," Kerri said.

"Yeah, she does," Jake agreed reluctantly. Grace Sinclair was lovely and seemed nice and she was probably in for a world of hurt thanks to Justin.

"Hopefully Justin will step up." Jeffrey

looked at the little girls still in their high chairs happily finishing their meals. "What a mess," he muttered under his breath.

What a mess, indeed. Jake's stomach knotted as he thought of the moment of realization on his brother's face and his ensuing race out of the kitchen.

He shouldn't be surprised. That's what Justin did best...make trouble and then run from whatever the consequences. Even though there was only a seventeen-minute difference in their ages, sometimes Jake felt as if his brother was seventeen years younger.

Jake had cleaned up plenty of Justin's problems in the past, but he wasn't running to the rescue this time. He couldn't. Justin was just going to have to suck it up and deal with the fact that he was now the father of three little girls.

"Maybe I should go check on her," Kerri said and started to get out of her chair.

"No, I'll go check. You stay here with the kids." Wearily Jake pulled himself out of his chair.

"Bye-bye," Bonnie said as Jake started toward the kitchen door.

For a moment he paused and stared at the three consequences of two adults' carelessness. It had to be difficult for a third-grade teacher to be single-handedly raising three babies. Hell, it would be difficult for any woman alone, no matter what her profession.

Despite her words to the contrary, Jake had no idea if Grace needed financial help or not. Surely just buying diapers and essentials for three little ones would be a hardship on a teacher's salary.

Girls need fathers in their lives. That's what

she'd said to him when she'd thought he was the daddy. Jake didn't know what little girls needed, but he'd always believed that he and his brothers would have been better off with far less father in their lives.

"Bye-bye," Bonnie said again, snapping him out of his momentary reverie.

He muttered a goodbye and then left the kitchen. Time would tell exactly what Grace needed from Justin and how his brother would step up to provide what she needed, what the little girls needed.

He was halfway to the front door when he heard Grace shriek from outside. With a burst of adrenaline he raced out the door. His heart nearly stopped when he saw her crumpled on the ground by the porch steps.

"Grace!" He rushed to her side as she sat up, her face unnaturally pale as she grabbed her left arm with her right. He glanced around but didn't see Justin, and his truck was gone.

"What happened?" he asked as he reached a hand out to help her up off the ground.

"It was stupid. I missed the step and fell." She winced as she got to her feet.

"What hurts?" he asked.

"I hit my shoulder." Her face was still bleached white even though she attempted a smile. "I'm sure it's fine." As she tried to drop it to her side she hissed in obvious pain and pulled it back up again.

"That doesn't look fine," Jake replied with a scowl.

"I'm sure I'll be okay. I just need to collect the girls and we'll all be on our way." They started up the stairs to the front door.

"I guess it didn't go so great with Justin?" he asked even though he knew the answer.

She shot him a glance and he was surprised to see tears brimming in her eyes. She quickly looked away, as if embarrassed. "He basically just screamed that I'd ruined his life and then got into his truck and peeled off down the road. Yes, I think it's safe to say that things didn't go so great."

"He doesn't handle surprises very well," Jake said as he opened the door for her. He cursed his natural impulse to make excuses for Justin. "I'm sure once he calms down he'll be more reasonable." At least that's what Jake hoped would happen. But he figured Justin had probably done what he always did when he got upset—headed directly to Tony's Tavern.

Grace slid through the door in front of him. "Once he *calms down and is more reasonable* he can call me or find me in Wichita. As soon as I pack up the girls, we'll be on our way back home."

He didn't try to change her mind. Maybe the best thing would be for her to head home and give him an opportunity to talk some sense into his brother.

This wasn't a speeding ticket that could be taken care of with the writing of a check. This wasn't a drunk and disorderly charge where Jake could talk the sheriff into not locking Justin up in jail for the night.

"Everything all right?" Kerri asked worriedly as they reentered the kitchen.

"Fine," Grace replied. "I want to thank you all for your wonderful hospitality, but it's time the girls and I get back on the road. If I leave now I'll be able to get home to Wichita before dark."

"Are you sure you wouldn't rather spend the

night here and get a fresh start in the morning?" Kerri asked as she got up from the table. "We certainly have plenty of room."

Jake watched Grace, who shook her head negatively. "Thanks for the offer, but I'd rather just get back home," she said.

Her cheeks hadn't regained any color. He didn't know if the paleness had to do with the situation or if it was the pain from her fall.

His question was answered the minute she tried to get Abby out of the high chair. Grace started to lift the child, but immediately cried out and grabbed her left shoulder instead.

"What happened?" Jeffrey asked as he jumped out of his chair and hurried to Grace's side.

"I took a little tumble in the yard." Her voice was filled with pain.

"Justin didn't push you, did he?" Kerri

asked, a touch of outrage in her voice. Jake looked at Kerri in surprise. As far as he knew his brother had never laid a finger on any woman, but of course he'd never found out he was the father of triplets before either.

"No, nothing like that," Grace replied hurriedly. "I just missed a step, stumbled and went down."

"We need to get you to the hospital and have that shoulder looked at," Jake said, deciding somebody had to take control of the situation. There was no way he could let her leave knowing she couldn't lift the little girls. It wouldn't even be safe for her to drive her car.

He expected Grace to protest. Instead, after a moment of hesitation, she nodded, which let him know that it had to be hurting her quite a bit.

"Maybe you're right. It's really painful."

Still she made no move. She gazed at her three daughters, who were happily smooshing and playing and eating what was left on their plates.

"Then let's go." Jake dug his truck keys out of his pocket. "The girls will be fine here with Kerri and Jeffrey."

"Absolutely," Kerri replied with a reassuring smile. "It will be good practice for us."

"I promise you, they'll be fine," Jake said to Grace. She held his gaze, as if trying to peer inside him to see if she could trust him. "Come on," he said with a touch of impatience. "You can decide what you want to do about heading home after the doctor takes a look at you."

He could tell she was reluctant to go, but it was obvious she was in a fair amount of pain. She was going to the hospital if he had to throw her over his shoulder and carry her there.

They didn't speak as she followed him out of the house and they got into his truck.

A new surge of irritation filled him. He shouldn't be the one taking her to the hospital. It should have been Justin. His brother should be the one taking care of the mother of his children, no matter what the circumstances.

"I'm so sorry," she finally said as he pulled out of the drive and onto the main road that would take them to Cameron Creek.

"Don't apologize. You didn't fall on purpose," he replied. He could smell her, the scent of a bouquet of wildflowers that was far too appealing.

"True, but the last thing I wanted was to be any kind of a bother to anyone." She leaned back against the seat. For a moment she looked so achingly vulnerable Jake wanted to reach out and touch her, assure her somehow that everything was going to be fine.

Instead he clenched the steering wheel more tightly. "Look, I know Justin behaved badly. But I meant it when I said once he's had time to digest everything I'm sure the two of you will be able to work something out."

"All I really wanted was for him to know about them and maybe spend some time with the girls, be a positive role model in their lives." She shifted positions and hissed in a breath, as if any kind of upper body movement caused her pain.

"You must have hit the ground pretty hard."

"I did. I have a gun in my pocket, and even though the safety was on, as I was falling I was afraid I'd hit the ground so hard it would pop off and somehow I'd shoot myself, so I twisted to make sure my shoulder and not my side took the brunt of the fall."

"A gun?" He looked at her in stunned surprise. She definitely didn't look like the gun-toting type. "Why on earth would you have a gun in your pocket?"

"I didn't know what kind of people you were. I wasn't even sure I'd find Justin here. I wasn't about to drive into a place where I'd never been before without some sort of protection for me and my girls. Besides, I got your address from a cyberfriend and my sister was afraid I might wind up at the home of some pervert sitting around in his underwear and stalking women over the internet."

"I'm definitely not a pervert, but if Jeffrey and Kerri weren't living with me, there might be times I'd sit around in my underwear," he replied with a wry grin.

He felt himself relaxing a bit, some of his irritation passing. None of this was her fault, and he'd be a jerk to punish her for his brother's actions or inactions.

He was rewarded with her smile, and her beauty with that gesture warming her features struck him square in the gut. He quickly focused his attention back on the road.

Okay, he could admit it to himself, he felt a little burn of physical attraction for Grace Sinclair. He shouldn't be surprised. She was a beautiful woman, and it had been over a year since Jake and the woman he'd been seeing for almost six months had called it quits. Just because Grace attracted him didn't mean there was a chance in hell that he'd follow through on it.

She was Justin's issue, not his. And the very last thing Jake wanted in his life at this moment or at any time in the future was anyone who might need him. The last thing he needed was another issue to solve. He was totally burned out in that area.

He slowed his speed as they entered the city limits of Cameron Creek. Unlike a lot of the small towns in Oklahoma that were dying slow, painful deaths, Cameron Creek was thriving and growing. There seemed to be no rhyme or reason for the anomaly other than the fact that the city council of Cameron Creek worked hard to make it a pleasant place to live. It also helped that on the south side of town was a large dog food factory that employed most of the people in the area.

"Hopefully I've just bruised it and it will be fine in an hour or two," she said as he parked in front of the attractive little hospital's emergency room entrance.

"You still have that gun in your pocket?" he asked as he shut off the engine. She nodded. She used her right hand to reach in her left pocket and pulled out the revolver. "It would probably be best if you didn't carry it into the emergency room. Do you mind if I lock it in the glove box?"

"You promise me you aren't a pervert?" she asked with a touch of teasing in her voice.

An unexpected burst of laughter escaped him. "I promise," he said as she offered him the gun. With it safely locked inside the glove box, they left the truck and headed through the emergency entrance.

Thankfully there was nobody in the waiting room and Grace was immediately whisked away to be seen by the doctor. Jake lowered himself into one of the waiting room chairs and tried to tamp down his aggravation with his brother.

There were times Jake dreamed of selling the ranch and leaving Oklahoma. There were days the thought of being on a deserted island all alone was infinitely appealing. But the vision was only appealing for a minute. He loved the ranch and would probably never leave.

Still, he'd thought that once he survived his childhood years life would get easier, but the death of his parents hadn't changed anything. His responsibilities had only gotten heavier.

He was tired, and the only thing he wanted now was for the doctor to fix up Grace so she could be on her way home. He'd encourage his brother to do the right thing and then Jake would wash his hands of the whole mess.

He wouldn't mind spending a little time with his nieces, eventually. But before that could happen Justin and Grace were going to have to figure things out. And that had nothing to do with him.

He'd spent most of his life shouldering responsibilities to make life easier on everyone else around him. Now what he wanted more than anything was just to be left alone.

It was almost an hour later that Dr. Wallington came out to greet him. Jake stood and shook the older man's hand. Dr. Wallington had been their family doctor for years.

"Grace wanted me to come out and let you know she's fine. X-rays showed no break, although her shoulder is severely sprained. I'm putting her in a sling to immobilize it for a couple of days and I've given her some pain medication. In the meantime she shouldn't do any driving or lifting and I've told her if it isn't better in three or four days she should come back in."

Jake smiled, nodded and thanked the doctor while inwardly cringing at the news. There was no way he could put Grace in her car with three babies to return home. She was going to need help, and plenty of it.

A weary resignation rose up inside him. All he'd wanted from life was a little peace and quiet, but any hope for that flew out the window. His life was about to be turned upside down with the invasion of three little girls and a woman who disturbed him in a way no woman ever had before.

Chapter 3

"Stupid, stupid, stupid," Grace muttered to herself as she waited for the nurse to return to the room to fit her with a sling. She'd been stupid to chase out of the house after Justin, and even more stupid to be so angry she'd managed to miss the first porch step and fall on her shoulder.

Now she was in a mess. The doctor had said she couldn't drive and she couldn't lift. How was she going to manage? The last thing she wanted to do was to ignore the doctor's advice and exacerbate the injury.

Tears suddenly burned at her eyes. This whole trip had been a nightmare. She'd been stupid to believe that there was a possibility of a happy ending for her babies, that she'd somehow walk away from here with a loving, caring man committed to being an integral part of their lives.

In her very first encounter with Justin she'd thought he was charming and hot, but now she realized he was just an immature hot-head.

She wanted to give him the benefit of the doubt. She wanted to believe that once the initial shock of the whole situation wore off, he'd step up and be a man. Be the father she wanted for her girls. But her first impression of him had definitely been a bad one.

In the meantime, she was going to have to leave this examining room and ask Jake, with his dark blue eyes and that edge of aloofness about him, if she could stay at his place for a couple of days until her shoulder healed enough that she could make it back home.

There was no way she could take the chance of trying to drive home alone, no way once she got there that she could take care of the girls. She certainly couldn't depend on Natalie. Her sister might be good for an hour or two of help here and there, but not the kind of care it would take for the next couple of days.

She'd have to depend on the kindness of virtual strangers and she hated that. The tears threatened to fall and she wasn't sure if they were caused by her situation, by Justin's reaction or the pain that radiated down her arm from her injured shoulder. She quickly swallowed against the tears as the nurse reappeared in the room.

Within minutes her arm was immobilized, and she'd called Natalie to let her know what was going on. Afterward she walked into the waiting room where Jake stood staring out the window. For a moment she didn't make a sound, just stared at his broad back.

He looked so solid. For a fleeting moment she wished he would have been the handsome cowboy at the wedding that night. It was a ridiculous thought. She knew no more about Jake than she did about his brother Justin. But what little she did know led her to believe that Jake would never find himself out of control, drunk in bed with a stranger. And he would have never torn out of a driveway after screaming to some woman that she'd ruined his life.

He whirled around as if he'd heard her thoughts, and he couldn't quite hide the scowl that had apparently ridden his features before he'd turned.

"Ah, there you are," he said smoothly as he approached her. "It looks as if you're going to be our houseguest for a few days. I've already called Jeff and Kerri to get things arranged at the house."

"I'm sure after a good night's rest I'll be fine to go home in the morning," she said as they left the hospital and walked outside.

"We'll see in the morning." He didn't sound too sure about her being capable of leaving that soon.

"I'm so sorry about this," she said when they were both back in his truck.

"You really have to stop apologizing." He smiled then and unexpected warmth fluttered in her chest. He had such a nice smile. "Accidents happen, Grace. We're all just going to have to figure out how to make the best of things."

"That's what I was trying to do by coming here. I'd hoped to take a difficult situation and somehow make it work in the best interests of my daughters." She paused for a long moment, and then continued, "I was a fool to come here." A touch of bitterness laced her voice.

"I'm hoping by tomorrow you and Justin will be able to sit down together and work things through."

"If today was any indication of the way one works things through with Justin then I don't think my body can take it," she replied drily.

He shot her a quick glance. "We'll just have to make sure you stay on your feet tomorrow."

"Tell me about him," she said. "What does Justin do for a living?"

Jake hesitated a minute. "He works for me at the ranch part-time."

That didn't sound great. She wondered what he did with his other time. "I'm assuming he isn't married. Does he have a girlfriend?"

Jake shot her a tight smile. "Justin dates a lot, although he's been seeing Shirley Caldwell for the last couple of months. She works as a waitress at a café in Cameron Creek."

"I really don't want to make any trouble for him." Grace frowned and tried to focus on the conversation instead of the excruciating pain that racked her arm each time she moved. Surely by morning it would be okay and she could get home.

"Let's just get you back to the ranch and settled in and we'll sort the rest of it out later."

They both fell silent for the remainder of the ride. What she'd wanted to ask him about his brother was if Justin was trustworthy and kind. Was he a good man who would make a good role model for his daughters? She didn't want to judge him based on their initial interaction earlier that day. She hoped Jake was right, that Justin's actions upon seeing her and the girls weren't indicative of who he was as a man, and once the shock wore off things would be fine.

For now there was nothing she could do but rest her arm and hope that by the morning she could get back home. What she wanted more than anything was to get back to the Johnson ranch and make sure her girls were okay.

She shot a quick glance at Jake and once

again couldn't imagine how she'd mistaken him for his brother. Although their features were basically the same, Jake's looked stronger, as if forged by a different metal than his brothers. Jake looked older and radiated a quiet confidence she found oddly sexy.

She moved her arm, welcoming the pain to banish any crazy thoughts about Jake that might enter her head. She released an exhausted sigh of relief as they pulled up in front of the house.

Kerri met them at the door. "You poor woman," she said to Grace. "Don't you worry about a thing. We're going to take good care of you and the babies until you're well enough to go home. I've got one of the guest rooms all ready for you, and Jeffrey got the old cribs out of the attic and has them set up in the room next to ours," Kerri continued as she led Grace into the kitchen.

"I hate being such an imposition," Grace said as she entered the kitchen to see the triplets once again playing on the floor with an array of plastic bowls and lids in front of them. The girls all smiled at the sight of their mother and continued playing as Grace sank down in one of the chairs at the table.

Thankfully the girls were used to being without Grace for hours in the day as she took them to day care while she worked. They were usually happy wherever they were as long as they were together.

Jeffrey and Jake came into the kitchen. Jeffrey sat at the table while Jake stood with his back against the counter, his gaze dark and enigmatic as he looked first at the children and then at Grace.

She could only imagine what was going on in his mind. He'd been invaded by unwanted children, by an unwanted woman. Was it any wonder he appeared rather grim?

"Don't look so worried," Kerri said to Grace. "We'll get them taken care of and all you need to be concerned with is getting that shoulder well."

Grace smiled at the woman gratefully. She certainly wouldn't be feeling as comfortable about things without Kerri here.

"Now, I'm going to make dinner," Kerri said.

"And you should take one of those pain pills the doctor gave you," Jake said to Grace.

She shook her head. "I'm fine. I really don't like to take pain pills. They make me groggy."

Jake pushed off the counter. "I'm heading out to the barn."

"Dinner in an hour," Kerri said.

He nodded and then left the kitchen. Once again Grace felt some of the tension ease out of her body. There was no question about it, something about Jake Johnson put her on edge. She felt a vague sense of disapproval wafting from him. Could she really blame him? For all he knew she was some kind of bimbo who made a habit of falling into bed with handsome cowboys.

He probably thought she was here for money despite her claims to the contrary. He had no reason to believe anything she'd told him.

They had a quiet dinner and then at about seven o'clock, with Jeffrey and Kerri's help, the girls were bathed, put into their pajamas and laid down in the cribs where they fell asleep almost immediately.

Jake had disappeared right after dinner, muttering that he was going into his office where he'd remained. With the girls asleep, Kerri showed Grace to the spare room and Jeffrey offered to bring in her suitcase and anything else she needed from her car.

The guest room was nice, decorated in shades of yellow and with a sliding glass door that led out to a small balcony. Grace stowed her things and by eight o'clock she, Kerri and Jeffrey sat in the living room. The television was on, but Grace's thoughts were far away from the drama unfolding on the screen.

In this single day her life had held enough drama to last her a lifetime. She was more than eager to get back to her home in Wichita, raise her daughters by herself and help her sister find her way through life.

Her shoulder throbbed with a pain that

made any real depth of thought next to impossible. She'd already decided that before she went to sleep that night she'd take one of those pain pills the doctor had given her. Hopefully the girls would sleep through the night as they usually did and Grace would feel well enough to head home the next day.

They all turned as the front door opened. Grace's stomach clenched as Justin walked in. His eyes widened slightly as he saw the sling she wore. "What happened?"

"I fell and hurt my shoulder," she replied. She wasn't sure if she should be happy or angry to see him again.

He looked at Kerri and Jeffrey. "Do you mind? Can I talk to her alone?"

Kerri looked at Grace, who nodded slightly. "Come on, Jeffrey, let's go into the kitchen and have a piece of pie."

Grace looked back at Justin. He seemed calm and contrite, although she thought she caught the scent of beer wafting from him.

"I'm sorry," he said once Kerri and Jeffrey had disappeared from the room. "About how I acted earlier. I was a real jerk and I truly do apologize."

She gave a curt nod, not exactly ready to accept his apology but at least willing to acknowledge it. He slid into the chair across from where she sat on the sofa.

"Man, what a freak-out." He released a sigh and raked a hand through his thick, dark hair. "So, how did you find me? I don't remember us exchanging too much personal information that night, although obviously we exchanged enough."

"Actually, I didn't find you. A friend of

mine did." She quickly explained to him about MysteryMom.

"Wow, it just gets freakier," he exclaimed when she was finished. "So, I got three kids."

"Three daughters. Justin, I don't care about child support if that's what you're worried about. I just thought you should know about them. I thought maybe you'd want to be a part of their lives." Her heart hurt in her chest as she watched his expression, as she clung to the belief that somehow, some way this man would step up.

"Can I see them?"

Her hope found a bit of purchase at this request, although she shook her head negatively. "They're sleeping right now. I really don't want them disturbed tonight. Unfortunately, with my shoulder injury I won't be going home for a day or two."

"Then why don't I plan on being here at ten in the morning and spend a little time with them." He stood from his chair. "And we can talk then about where things go from here."

The tentative hope blossomed and she offered him a smile. "I'd like that."

"Then I'll see you at ten tomorrow." He disappeared out the front door and Grace breathed a sigh of relief. Maybe everything was going to be okay after all.

She turned to see Jake standing in one of the doorways nearby, apparently the door that led into his private study. "You were right," she said. "He just needed some time to process it all, I guess." She smiled.

"I'm just heading up to my room so I'll say good-night," he said.

"Good night, Jake, and thank you for everything. Justin is going to be here around ten tomorrow to get to know the girls, so it looks as though things are going to be just fine."

"Let's hope so," he said, his eyes once again dark and unreadable. There was something in his tone and in the darkness of his gaze that made Grace realize maybe she shouldn't get her hopes up too high.

It was ten-thirty the next morning and there was still no sign of Justin. Jake wasn't surprised. What did surprise him was the ping of compassion in his heart as he watched Grace standing at the front window looking outside.

She'd been there for the last twenty minutes, her demeanor slowly shifting from eager anticipation to unmistakable discouragement.

The girls were playing on a blanket on the living room floor, surrounded by toys and any other item in the house that Kerri thought they might enjoy and wouldn't hurt them. Kerri had helped get them up and out of bed, fed and dressed in cute little outfits he suspected had been specifically chosen to meet their daddy.

"You want a cup of coffee or something?" he finally asked.

Grace whirled around, green eyes wide. "Oh, I didn't know you were there. No thanks, I'm fine." She turned back to face the window. "He's apparently running late."

"Justin is one of those people who would be late to his own funeral." Jake wasn't sure he believed his brother would show up at all. Thank goodness the babies were young enough not to know that already they'd been let down by the man who had fathered them. The one man in the world they should be able to depend on. Jake feared it wouldn't be the last time.

"How's the shoulder this morning?" he asked.

Once again she turned from the window and this time took several steps away and sat in a nearby chair. "I think it's a little better," she replied, but as she tried to move it to show him how much better it was a spasm of pain crossed her features.

"I think maybe you just told me a little fib," he noted.

She hesitated a moment and then flashed him a quick smile. "Maybe," she admitted. "Actually, I think it's worse this morning than it was last night."

"That doesn't surprise me. I've always heard the second day of an injury is the worst." He should be outside, riding the ranch, checking fencing, doing a thousand chores that awaited his hands. But he'd been unable to leave her alone standing at the window waiting for a man who might not show up until evening.

What he shouldn't be doing was standing there admiring the play of sunshine in her hair, enjoying how her yellow T-shirt, which made her green eyes even more vivid, clung to her breasts.

She got up from the chair and returned to the window. "Surely he'll be here any minute now," she said softly.

He heard the hope in her voice, the same hope that he'd heard the night before, and it disturbed him. He didn't want her depending on Justin for anything. Jake would like to believe that for once in his life, for something so important, Justin would step up. But Jake had been burned too many times. He knew about the hope Grace felt, and he knew the bitter taste left behind when it faded away.

He stepped up to the window next to her and was engulfed by the clean, sweet scent of her, a scent that instantly created a faint pleasant fire in the pit of his stomach.

But he'd also noticed the tiny fatigue lines that radiated from her eyes, the slender lines of her body that indicated a woman who had little time to eat or sleep. She probably wasn't taking care of herself the way she should. How could she with a full-time job and triplets to raise all alone?

"He's here!" she exclaimed at the same time Jake saw his brother's truck pull into the driveway. "Oh, it looks as if he's brought somebody with him."

As the truck drew closer to the door Jake could see that Justin had Shirley with him.

Jake swallowed a string of curses. Why on earth would Justin bring with him the woman he was dating, a hot-tempered, overly jealous drama queen with big hair and bigger breasts?

Justin and Shirley both got out of the truck. Shirley was dressed in a bright pink blouse, a pair of short shorts that exposed overly tanned legs and overly steep, sparkly high heels.

The two of them spoke for a moment and then Shirley got back into the truck and Justin headed for the front door. Jake was grateful his brother at least had the sense to leave Shirley cooling her heels outside. Although the odds of Justin spending any quality time with the triplets weren't good.

Grace met Justin at the door and the bright smile she gave him ached inside Jake; just below the heady scent of her he smelled disappointment in the air.

"Hey," Justin greeted her, not quite meeting her eyes. "Uh, something's come up and I really don't have time to hang around here today. I was wondering if maybe we could set something up for tomorrow?" He glanced over his shoulder to the woman in the pickup who appeared to be glaring daggers at Grace.

"Justin, you know where I am. I'll be here probably through tomorrow, so let's just leave it loose and I'll see you when I see you," Grace replied, a faint weariness in her voice.

He gave her a grateful glance, never making eye contact with Jake. "Great, thanks. Then I guess I'll talk to you tomorrow." He turned and ran back toward the truck.

For a long moment Grace remained at the front door, and Jake dreaded seeing the depth of the disappointment in her lovely green eyes when she turned around. "So much for that," she said softly as she walked away from the door. She offered Jake a tentative smile. "I guess the good news is his girlfriend didn't get out of the truck and try to beat me up." She touched the sling on her arm. "I'm not exactly on top of my game right now."

The thought of the elegant Grace involved in a girl fight was so ludicrous a small burst of laughter escaped Jake's lips. It surprised him. He couldn't remember the last time he'd actually laughed out loud.

Unfortunately the laughter lasted only a moment and then they faced each other awkwardly. "I've got work outside to do," he said, realizing that he'd once again been admiring the shine of her hair in the sunlight, vaguely wondering if it would feel as silky as it looked.

"And I should check with Kerri to see if I can help with lunch." She stepped aside so he could go out the door.

As he headed for the barn he carried with him a vague irritation at Justin and a faint simmer of something quite different for Grace. Both emotions were equally unwanted.

Despite the fact that she'd obviously gone through the pregnancy and the first ten months of the triplets' lives pretty much on her own, there was a soft vulnerability about her that called to that old, familiar protective instinct in him, a protective instinct he'd been trying to banish for the past year.

He knew the ranch hands he employed would be out in the fields. But at least once a day Jake headed out on horseback to check the livestock and just enjoy the fresh air and alone time.

Alone time. Jake didn't feel as though he'd been truly alone since the moment of his conception. And it was what he longed for more than anything. As much as he loved Jeff and Kerri, he couldn't wait for their house to be finished and to have the house to himself. He just wanted the time to come when nobody needed anything from him ever again.

Still, as he saddled his horse his thoughts returned to Grace. Maybe things would have been easier if she was more like Justin's usual women. Justin's normal types were tough, life-weary women who knew the score where he was concerned. They knew how to fight for what they wanted and they didn't always fight fair. They also knew to expect nothing from Justin and that's usually what they ended up with where he was concerned.

Grace had a quiet elegance about her. She worked as a schoolteacher, and he'd believed her when she'd told him she wasn't the type to fall into bed easily with any man.

Minutes later he was racing across the pasture, shoving thoughts of the beautiful brown-haired woman out of his head. When his parents had died and left this large ranch to the three young men, Jake knew it would never work with three cooks and no chef.

He knew that Jeffrey had never wanted to be a rancher. He preferred working with numbers, loved being an accountant and had no desire to have anything to do with the ranch except help keep the books.

Justin didn't have the work ethic necessary to keep it a successful, functioning business and so Jake had offered to buy them both out. They'd banged out the details, worked with the bank and a lawyer and now the land was his, except for the plot where Jeffrey and Kerri were building their place.

Both Justin and Jeffrey got a payment each month from the profits the ranch made and would do so until their part of the inheritance was paid off.

He rode until just after noon and then headed back to the house for lunch. The three little girls were already in their high chairs, chattering and taking turns laughing as if enjoying each other's conversation.

"Are they always so happy?" he asked as he walked over to the sink to wash up.

"Pretty much all the time," Grace said. She was already seated at the table while Kerri stood at the stove stirring a big pot of vegetable soup. "The only time they're at all fussy is if they get overly tired."

"That's the only time I get fussy," Kerri said with a laugh. She began to ladle the soup into a large tureen.

Lunch was a quiet meal. Grace seemed pulled into herself, her gaze lingering often on her three daughters as they ate their finger food.

Jake tried not to notice the sadness that wafted from Grace, a sadness he knew his brother was responsible for. *Not my problem,* he reminded himself over and over again. But when lunch was finished and the girls were down for their naps, the sight of Grace sitting alone on the sofa in the living room made it impossible for him to just leave her there and disappear into his study.

"How about a walk outside for a little fresh

air?" he said to her. "I'll show you around the place."

She glanced toward the stairs and then looked at her watch. "Okay, that sounds good. The girls usually nap for about an hour and a half and they just went down."

"I'll let Kerri know we're going out. She can keep an ear open for any of the girls waking up," he said. It took him only a moment to alert Kerri of their intention, and then he and Grace stepped out on the porch into the midafternoon spring sunshine.

"Ever been on a ranch?" he asked.

"No, I've always been an urban girl," she replied. "Although I sometimes take my class to a petting farm in Wichita for a field trip. Looks as though you have a lot of land."

He nodded. "It's almost six hundred acres.

I use some of it for crops, but most of it is for cattle."

"You run it all alone?"

They walked in the direction of the barn in the distance, the sun warm and the air spiced with the scents of flowers and pasture. "No, I've got several men who help out."

"I haven't seen anyone around."

"They're usually out in the fields by this time of the day. I'm sure if you're here long enough you'll eventually see them."

"No offense, but I hope I'm not here that long," she replied.

"Already tired of our company?" he said, half teasing.

"You all have been wonderful, but I came here with a specific purpose in mind and now that I've accomplished what I set out to do, I'm eager to get home."

And he wanted her gone, he reminded himself, although it was difficult to maintain that feeling when she looked so beautiful and smelled so good. "You didn't exactly accomplish what you wanted," he said.

A tiny frown danced in the center of her forehead. "Your brother is obviously not cut out to be much of a family man." She looked up at him. "What about you? You have a girlfriend with plans to marry and fill this big place with lots of children?"

"No," he replied firmly. "Never. I know it sounds crazy, but with my brothers I feel as if I've been parenting most of my life. Once Kerri and Jeffrey move out, I am looking forward to being alone. The last thing I want is the responsibility of a wife or kids." He realized he sounded harsh and he tempered his words with a smile. "But that doesn't mean I'm not ready to step up as an uncle."

"I appreciate that. I'd just hoped..." She allowed her voice to trail off.

Jake didn't know how to reply. He couldn't make his brother into the man she wanted him to be, although heaven knew he'd tried over the years to make him into some kind of a responsible man.

At that moment his cell phone rang. He pulled it from his pocket and realized it was a call he had to take and he needed to be in his study in order to refer to some documents. "I'll call you right back," he said to the man on the other end of the line.

"I'm sorry, I've got to get back inside," he said to Grace. "That was a business call I need to return. Shall we head back?"

"If you don't mind, I think I'll walk around

a little bit longer. It feels good to be out here in the fresh air and sunshine."

Once again that protectiveness surged up inside him. She looked lost, and he knew the disappointment of the morning with Justin weighed heavily in her heart. He steeled his own heart against her. "Okay, then I'll just see you inside in a few minutes."

As he walked back toward the house, he fought the impulse to turn and get one more look at her. He told himself again he wasn't going to get sucked into this drama, that Justin and Grace were going to have to figure it all out on their own.

That protective streak Jake had in him had resulted in many a beating throughout his youth from their father, who had handed out corporal punishment for any infringement, slight or imagined. Jake had taken more than one beating for Justin, and he was determined to never take another on behalf of either of his brothers.

It took him nearly twenty minutes to take care of the business that needed attending. He was just leaving his study when he heard the unmistakable sound of a gunshot.

What the hell?

He raced to the front window and looked out, stunned to see Grace with her back pressed against the side of the barn. Another shot split the air and it was immediately obvious to him that somebody was shooting at her. The shots were coming from a thickly wooded area on the right of the property.

Jake's heart leapt in his throat as he raced back into his study and grabbed his gun from his desk drawer. Somebody was shooting at Grace. It didn't make sense. His mind couldn't wrap around it. As another shot exploded he only hoped he could get outside before whoever it was managed to kill her.

Chapter 4

Grace pressed against the rough wood of the side of the barn, terror clawing up her throat as another bullet splintered the wood precariously close to where she stood.

Her brain had stopped functioning when the first bullet had whizzed by her. If she hadn't heard the explosion of the gun she would have assumed the loud buzz was an annoying insect too close to her ear.

When she'd realized what was happening she'd slammed herself against the barn in an effort to make herself a more difficult target. If she could, she'd push herself right through the wood and into the barn itself.

Who was shooting at her and why? None of this made any sense. But there was nobody else around, no way to mistake that those bullets were intended for her.

She cursed her bright yellow T-shirt that made her an easy target as her eyes darted around frantically seeking some sort of a safe escape.

Her heart pounded so loudly in her ears she couldn't hear anything else. Why was this happening? What was going on? The sight of Jake barreling out of the front door with a gun in his hand forced a sob of relief to escape her lips.

He fired several shots into the woods where the original bullets had come from as he ran toward her. Jeffrey appeared on the porch with a rifle and he began to fire into the woods as well, providing cover for Jake as he approached where she stood.

Jake slammed against the barn next to her. "You all right?" he asked, his voice a terse snap of tension.

She gave a curt nod, unable to find her voice. Her terror had stolen it clean away from her.

"We're going to get you back into the house," he said, his eyes narrowed to dangerous-looking slits. There had been no more gunfire coming from the woods since he'd appeared.

"I'm afraid to move," she finally managed to reply.

"We need to move," he replied. "Did you see anyone?" he asked, not taking his gaze from the woods.

"No, I just felt the first bullet buzz by my head and I ran, but I didn't know where to run to." A tremble tried to take hold of her body but she fought against it, knowing she couldn't give in to her fear until she was safe and sound.

She certainly felt safer with Jake by her side and with Jeffrey on the front porch, but someplace out there was somebody who had apparently just tried to kill her not once, not twice, but three times.

There could be no other explanation for what had happened. Any one of those bullets could have hit her...killed her...and she wasn't safe yet. They still had to get from the barn back to the house.

Several men appeared on horseback, rifles pulled and faces grim. "The cavalry," Jake muttered beneath his breath.

One of the men pulled up in front of Grace and Jake, providing an effective barrier. "We heard gunfire," he said. He was a big man, with shoulders as wide as a mountain and a paunch belly to match, but his eyes were dark and dangerous as he gazed first at Grace then at Jake.

"It came from the woods over there. Maybe you and the boys can go check it out while I get Grace safely back into the house," Jake said.

The cowboy gave a nod of his head and then he and the other two took off riding toward the woods. "Can you run?" Jake asked her.

"Not as fast as usual with my arm in this sling, but I'll do the best I can," she replied. She'd do whatever she could to get away from this barn and into the house.

Her babies. She needed to be with her

babies. She needed to kiss their plump cheeks, smell their baby sweetness and hug them tight.

"I'm going to wrap my arm around you," he said. "And then we're going to go as fast as we can to the house. Ready?"

He put his arm around her. For a moment she wanted to bury herself against him, to meld into the hard safety of his arms, to lose herself in his scent of sunshine and woodsy cologne.

"Ready," she murmured.

They took off and it was the most terrifying run Grace had ever experienced. With each step she expected a bullet to pierce through her back, to hit her body and slam her into the ground. And with each step her shoulder jarred, shooting pain through her and making her wonder if they'd ever reach the safety of the house.

All she could think about were her babies. If she died who would take care of them? Natalie certainly wasn't at a place in her life where she would be a fit parent. Justin definitely wasn't an option. Grace had to get back to the house safe and sound.

Jake used his bigger body as a shield. When they reached the porch and stumbled past Jeffrey and into the house, Grace wrapped her good arm around Jake's neck and clung to him as tears of fear and relief mingled together and finally erupted.

He remained stiff and unyielding for a long moment and then his arms went around her waist and he held her as tight as her slinged arm would allow.

"It's all right. You're okay now." His deep

voice reached inside her and soothed some of the jagged fear that still spiked through her as one of his hands slid up and down her back in a soft caress.

She buried her face in the front of his T-shirt as the tears fell freely. Someplace in the very back of her mind she recognized she liked the way he smelled, she liked the feel of his strong body so close to hers.

She didn't cry for long, but after the tears had stopped she was reluctant to leave his embrace. He felt so solid, so capable, and she hadn't realized until this moment how desperately she'd hungered for a man's embrace. For just a moment to be able to lean on somebody, anybody other than herself.

As Jeffrey came through the front door, she reluctantly released her hold on Jake and stepped away from him. Kerri grabbed her by the arm and led her to the sofa. Grace sank down and allowed the shudder that had threatened earlier to work through her.

"What on earth is going on around here?" Kerri asked, obviously distraught as she moved from Grace to her husband's side.

Everyone looked at Grace. Her shoulder ached, her heart raced and she still couldn't wrap her mind around what had just happened. "I don't know. I was just walking, enjoying the fresh air and sunshine. I heard the gunshot at almost the same time I felt the whiz of a bullet go by my head."

She began to tremble, the motion causing her shoulder to ache more and bringing with it a headache that screamed across the back of her skull. "At first I didn't realize what was happening, but when I did, I didn't know what to do. So I pressed against the side of the barn and then it was as if I was pinned there. Whoever it was kept firing. I thought I was going to be killed." She was rambling, her mouth working almost faster than her brain.

"Call the sheriff," Jake said to Kerri, who immediately went into the kitchen to use the phone in there.

A knock at the door whirled Jake around, his gun still drawn. Grace felt her breath catch painfully in her chest in frightening anticipation of more trouble. She relaxed as the cowboy Jake had sent to the woods came through the door.

"Somebody was out there," he said in a deep, booming voice. "Looks like whoever it was had been there for a while. The grass was tamped down and a blanket of some sort had been spread out."

"A blanket?" Grace stared at him in horror.

That implied somebody had been sitting out there just waiting for her to make an appearance, just waiting to put a bullet through her.

"The sheriff is on his way," Kerri said as she came back into the living room.

"By the way, Grace, this is Jimbo Watkins, my ranch manager. Jimbo, this is Grace Sinclair, a visitor here on the ranch," Jake said.

Jimbo tipped his black cowboy hat. "You brought some nasty critters with you when you arrived here from wherever you came from?"

"Wichita. And, no, I don't even know any nasty critters," Grace said, aware of the slight edge of hysteria in her voice. She was a schoolteacher, for crying out loud. She didn't know people who laid in wait to shoot a helpless woman. She knew eight-year-olds who had trouble with math and talked out of turn.

"Me and the boys will check out the rest of the property, but I'd say whoever was there is probably long gone by now," Jimbo said.

"You find anything else you come let me know," Jake said.

With another tip of his hat to Grace and Kerri, Jimbo left the house.

"Could this have been some sort of a mistake?" Grace finally ventured. "You know, a hunter taking some wild shots?"

"Honey, you *are* from the city," Kerri said drily.

"This was no mistake," Jake replied. His dark blue eyes lingered on Grace. "This isn't hunting season and there's no way anyone could confuse you with a wild turkey or a deer."

"So somebody just tried to kill me." The words fell from Grace's mouth and hung in the air as she stared at the people around her, hoping somebody would negate her words or at least somehow make it all make sense.

Instead, she heard a cry from upstairs and knew that the triplets were awake from their naps. "Go on, I'll let you know when the sheriff arrives," Jake said to Grace and Kerri.

As the two women climbed the stairs, Kerri grabbed hold of Grace's hand. "I can't imagine how frightened you must have been," she said as she squeezed Grace's fingers. "Nothing like this has ever happened before."

"I feel like it's all a horrible dream," Grace replied.

"It has to have been some sort of terrible mistake," Kerri replied as she dropped Grace's hand.

Only the sight of Abby's, Bonnie's and Casey's sweet little faces grinning at her over the tops of the cribs could finally calm some of the fear that had iced Grace's heart for what seemed like forever. "Hey, girls," she greeted them with a forced bright smile.

It took several minutes to change diapers, and with Abby and Casey on Kerri's hips and Bonnie riding Grace's good side, they went back down the stairs.

By the time they had the girls happily settled on the floor with toys surrounding them, the sheriff had arrived.

Sheriff Greg Hicks was a tall, gray-haired man with kind brown eyes and a deep cleft in his chin. "Would you get a load of these little beauties," he said with a look at the girls after Jake had made the introductions. "They're like peas in a pod and cute as buttons."

"Thank you," Grace said, noticing that

Bonnie was grinning and batting her eyelashes at Jake, obviously flirting as usual.

"Now, what's this I hear about a shooting taking place out here?" Sheriff Hicks asked as he looked at everyone standing around in the room.

Jake gestured them all to chairs. Grace found herself on the sofa next to him, and the memory of being in his strong arms played in her head. She had never felt so safe in her entire life as she had in those moments with his arms wrapped around her and his heart beating next to her own. For a wistful moment she wanted that again, that feeling of safety while standing in his strong arms.

"Grace and I were taking a walk outside when I got a phone call I needed to attend to in my study," Jake began. "It was a supplier and I needed to order some things. I had the list on my desk."

Grace picked up the story. "Jake asked me to head inside with him, but I told him I wanted to walk a little bit more and enjoy the sunshine and fresh air."

As she told the sheriff about the gunshots her heart began to beat faster and her throat went achingly dry as she thought of those moments when she was so certain she was about to be killed. "I've never been so scared in my entire life."

"I had some of my men check out the area in the woods where the gunfire came from. Jimbo told me it looks as if somebody had a blanket out there and was hanging around, maybe camping or something."

"You haven't seen anyone unusual around the place?" Hicks asked Jake.

He shook his head. "Nobody."

"Anybody around here have a beef with you?" Sheriff Hicks asked Grace.

"I don't know anyone around here," she replied. "I live in Wichita. This is my first time to the area, and I only just arrived yesterday." She paused a moment and averted her gaze from Jake. "Of course, it could have been Justin. He wasn't real happy to see me when I arrived here with his daughters."

Sheriff Hicks looked at her in surprise at the same time she heard Kerri gasp and felt Jake tense next to her in obvious protest.

"I can't imagine Justin doing anything like this," Sheriff Hicks said dubiously, "but I'll check it out. It's probably more likely a drifter who thought you were getting too close to where he'd been camped."

Grace had a crazy image in her head of

the Johnson family circling the wagons to protect one of their own against an intruder. And there was no question in her mind that she and her daughters were the intruders. No matter how nice these people had been to her, she was really on her own.

"Justin wouldn't do something like this," Jake exclaimed as he leapt to his feet the moment Sheriff Hicks walked out the front door. "I know my brother, and he might be a lot of things, but he's definitely not a cold-blooded killer." He glared at Grace as his stomach churned with anxiety.

"Well, I don't know him," she replied with strain in her voice. "Although I've certainly been trying to get to know him." She raised her chin as she returned his glare. "I'd be a fool not to mention his name to the sheriff given what's happened with him since I arrived here."

Bonnie crawled over to Jake and grabbed hold of his pants leg. She wobbled to her feet and raised her arms, obviously wanting to be picked up. Grace jumped off the sofa and hurried to the little girl, trying to wrangle her up in her arms one-handed. It was obvious from the awkwardness of her effort and the pain that spasmed across her face that her bad shoulder made it impossible.

Jake bent down, picked the child up and drew a deep breath to steady himself. "Look, I know Justin has behaved badly, but there's no way anyone can make me believe that he was out there in the woods trying to shoot you." Bonnie grabbed his nose with one hand and patted his face with the other.

He realized at that moment it was impossible to sustain any kind of anger with a ten-month-old giggling in your arms and squeezing your nose in delight. Besides, he wasn't really angry at Grace, he was angry with Justin for putting himself in the position to even be a suspect in a shooting. He was livid that a guest at his home had been nearly killed by an unknown assailant.

"Maybe you weren't the specific target," he finally said.

She frowned. "What does that mean?"

"Maybe it's just as Sheriff Hicks suggested. If it was a drifter or somebody who had set up some kind of makeshift camp, he might have shot at anyone he thought threatened his space." It was a stretch and Jake knew it, but none of it made any sense as far as he was concerned. No matter how he stretched his imagination he couldn't put this on his brother. Justin just couldn't be responsible for this.

"So what now?" Grace asked. There was something in her expression that told him she was taking a secret delight in the fact that Bonnie was now pulling the hairs in one of his eyebrows.

"We wait and see what Sheriff Hicks can find out," he replied. And personally he hoped to hell his brother had a good alibi for the time of the shooting.

At that moment Grace's cell phone rang. She pulled it from her pocket and answered. "How did that happen?" she asked after a minute. The frown that had already ridden her forehead deepened. "Okay, whatever. There's a credit card in the top drawer of my dresser underneath my camisoles. Take it and use it, but just for what you need and then put it back where you got it. Okay, yes, I love you, too."

Jake set Bonnie back on the floor, trying to dispel the thought of Grace in a camisole from his mind. The visual image that had instantly sprung into his head was as sexy as it was unwanted.

"Everything okay?" he asked.

She sighed. "Everything is as usual. My sister, Natalie, has a small trust fund and gets a monthly allowance, but somehow there's always more month than there is money for her. Anyway, it's taken care of for now."

"You didn't tell her what happened."

"There's no point in worrying her about all this. It's not as if she can do anything about it from Wichita." She released a sigh of obvious frustration. "Look, I didn't mean to throw your brother under the bus, but, under the circumstances, it would have been foolish of me not to mention him."

Kerri and Jeffrey had drifted out of the room, as if not wanting to be caught in the middle of any argument that might be brewing between Jake and Grace.

Jake didn't want to argue. He sat in the chair across from her and released a weary sigh. The adrenaline that had pumped through him when he'd seen Grace pinned against the barn had disappeared, leaving him confused and upset about everything that had happened.

"I know," he replied. "And it was the right thing to do."

There was a moment of awkward silence between them. Once again his head filled with a vision of her in a sexy, silky red camisole. He was grateful when she broke the silence.

"You know, it was a near-death experience that made me decide it was the right thing to do to find Justin in the first place," she said.

Jake looked at her in surprise. "What do you mean?"

Her cheeks flushed a delicate pink. "It probably doesn't sound like much now, but two days before I left Wichita to come here, I was on my way home from the grocery store. It was after dark, and Natalie was watching the girls while they slept so I could make a fast run to get some milk and a few other items. Anyway, I was on the way home and a car forced me off the road. I went down an embankment and it was only by the grace of God that the car didn't flip over and kill me."

"That's terrible," he said, surprised that the thought of her getting hurt created a tight band of pressure across his chest. He glanced at the triplets playing on the blanket. "And thank God they weren't with you."

She nodded. "Thank God is right."

"What did you do?"

"I was shaken up badly, but thankfully not hurt. The car had no real damage and the only result was groceries had spilled all over the backseat."

"Did you call the police?"

"No. There was really no point. I didn't get a good look at the car that forced me off the road and it was long gone by the time I finally pulled myself together. I managed to get back on the road and drive home and that was that. But that night I decided life was too short and too unpredictable and it was time I make contact with Justin."

Jake leaned back in his chair. "It doesn't make any sense—the shooting, I mean. First and foremost, I don't believe my brother is capable of trying to shoot you or anyone else. But, aside from that, it wouldn't make sense for him to do that. You being dead doesn't change the fact that he's their father. In fact, your death would only put more responsibility on him."

She raised a hand to the back of her neck and rubbed, as if trying to ease a tension headache. "That's true. I just need to get home. I need to take the girls and get back to Wichita," she murmured, more to herself than to him.

"But we both know that's not an option right now," he reminded her with a pointed glance at her shoulder. He stared out the window, unable to look at her and not remember how she'd felt in his arms.

Soft and yielding, she'd filled him with a

heat that had him instantly responding to her. Her hair had smelled slightly fruity, mingling with the floral scent of her, and when she'd stopped crying he'd been almost reluctant to let her go.

He definitely didn't want a woman in his life permanently, but that didn't mean he wouldn't mind one occasionally.

Just not Grace.

Definitely not Grace.

"Look, what I'm really hoping is that this is all some sort of weird mistake, that it was some delusional drifter on the property or a drunk cowboy just popping off his weapon," he said, forcefully pulling his thoughts away from their brief physical contact.

"Do those kinds of things happen a lot around here?" she asked, one of her perfectly arched pale eyebrows raised dubiously.

"No, they don't," he admitted. "But that doesn't mean it can't happen." He got up from the chair, feeling the need to distance himself from her.

"I'm going to go out and talk to my men. Maybe one of them indiscriminately shot off a couple of rounds and now is too embarrassed to admit to it."

What he really wanted to do was get hold of Justin and find out where he'd been when this whole thing had gone down, he thought as he walked to the porch. Although he couldn't imagine his brother having anything to do with what had happened, there was a tiny part of him that knew when Justin had a few beers in him almost anything was possible. But surely not this, his heart rebelled.

Finally, what he needed was some distance from Grace and the little girls. The triplets filled the house with a joyous noise he wasn't accustomed to, and Grace filled his head with thoughts—very dangerous thoughts.

Never in all his years had he been attracted to any woman Justin had brought around, and yet he was intensely attracted to Grace.

A couple of days, he told himself. A couple more days and they'd all be gone, back to where they'd come from, back to a life that had very little to do with his.

Things would be much easier when she went back to Wichita. He was far too conscious of her on a physical level, drawn to her in a way that was completely undesirable.

He pulled his cell phone from his pocket and punched in Justin's phone number, unsurprised when the call went directly to Justin's voice mail.

He turned at the sound of the door opening

and gave a tight smile to Jeffrey, who stepped out on the porch next to him. "Did you get in touch with him?" Jeffrey gestured to the cell phone Jake still held in his hand.

"No, it went straight to voice mail." Jake pocketed the phone and stared at the barn in the distance. No matter how many times he worked the events of the last couple of hours through his brain he couldn't make sense of it.

"He wouldn't do something like this. It doesn't make any sense," Jake said in frustration.

"When has anything Justin done made any sense?" Jeffrey countered drily.

"Yeah, but this is different than borrowing money or getting drunk or running up a bunch of traffic tickets. Grace could have been seriously hurt. She could have been killed." Jake's stomach muscles tightened. "If I find out he was behind this, then I'll wash my hands of him. I mean it," he said at Jeffrey's dubious look.

"You've carried him for a long time, Jake. Sooner or later he's got to stand on his own." Jeffrey clapped Jake on the shoulder. "And now to something else that's not going to make your day. You do remember that Kerri and I are leaving tomorrow for Topeka for a couple of days?"

Jake stared at his brother in horror as the full impact of his words struck. He knew better than to ask his brother to postpone the trip. It had been planned for months, an anniversary celebration at a bed-and-breakfast that was almost impossible to get reservations at.

With Kerri and Jeffrey gone, that meant

Jake would be alone in the house with Grace. He'd be alone with a woman with three little girls, an arm in a sling and, worst-case scenario, a murderer after her who had missed once, but might not be done trying.

Chapter 5

Grace sat on the edge of the bed in the guest room and stared out the sliding glass door that led to a small balcony. They had finished a quiet, tense dinner and then she and Kerri had gotten the girls into bed. She'd excused herself for an early night, just wanting to go to sleep and put all the troubling thoughts away for a while. But sleep had proved elusive.

Her shoulder hurt more tonight than it had since she'd fallen, and she knew there was no way she could make the drive home the next day. But it was the ache in her heart that made her feel half-sick.

Was it possible that the man who had fathered her daughters had tried to kill her? Jake certainly didn't believe so. He'd been adamant in his defense of Justin. There had been no word from the sheriff since he'd left the house and no sign or contact from Justin himself.

What she'd like to do was open the sliding door and step outside, get a breath of the fresh scent of night air in hopes it would settle her thoughts. But she was afraid. What if the shooter was still out there, just waiting for another opportunity to get to her? She'd make herself a perfect target out on the balcony.

Grace's mother had been a strong woman who had no tolerance for weakness of any kind, and Grace had tried to live up to that, but at the moment she felt weak and vulnerable and utterly alone.

She decided to call Natalie, who rarely went to bed before dawn, even though she knew there would be little comfort there. Natalie was always in the midst of her own drama. It was Grace who was usually fixing Natalie's life, not the other way around. In any case, the call went to Natalie's voice mail.

Although she didn't leave a message about the shooting, she did say that it had been a mistake to come here, that it was obvious being a father was the last thing in the world Justin wanted and that he'd probably never want to be part of the girls' lives. She explained that it would be another couple of days before she got home but that the trip had certainly been a waste of time where Justin was concerned.

Enough self-pity, she thought when she hung up. Maybe if she went downstairs and got a glass of milk or something it would help her sleep. She'd taken the sling off when she'd gotten into bed, finding it cumbersome. With difficulty she pulled on the red-and-black silk robe that matched her nightgown.

The house was dark and quiet as she left the bedroom. She slid into the room next door where a night-light gave off enough illumination for her to check each crib and see that the girls were all sleeping peacefully.

She stood for a long moment by each crib, her heart swelling in her chest with love. All she'd really wanted was for the girls to know their father and him to know them. She'd hoped that Justin would be the kind of man who would embrace the girls, a man she could be confident would take her babies and care for them if anything ever happened to her. Now she certainly wasn't going to leave here with that confidence. He didn't seem to have any real interest in even getting to know the girls. She just had to make sure she stayed alive and well until the triplets were adults.

Leaving the room as quietly as she'd entered, she made her way down the darkened hall to the stairway. From the living room she saw the glow of a small lamp on.

She followed the glow and found Jake seated in a chair. "Oh, I didn't know anyone else was still awake," she said as she self-consciously held the robe closer around her neck with her good hand.

"I couldn't sleep. Looks as though you're suffering from the same affliction." He gestured her toward the sofa. She noticed he had a glass of amber liquid in his hand. "Scotch," he said. "Would you like one?"

"No thanks. Contrary to what happened the night of Sally's wedding with a bottle of champagne, I'm really not much of a drinker." She sat on the sofa.

"Neither am I," he admitted and set the glass on the end table next to him. "I just occasionally like the taste of a little good Scotch. Sheriff Hicks called earlier."

Grace sat up straighter, trying to staunch the pain the motion created in her shoulder. "And?"

"And apparently there has been a drifter in the area. He stole some clothing from Rebecca Castor's clothesline and she chased him off with her broom. He was also apparently sleeping in Burt Kent's barn off and on. Several people around the area have seen him and told the sheriff he appears to be mentally unstable."

"So, it could have been him who took those shots at me." She wanted to believe it. She desperately wanted to believe that it had been anyone but Justin.

"It's possible. At least that's what Sheriff Hicks believes happened, although nobody who has caught sight of him has seen him with a weapon. Hicks and his men are trying to hunt him down, and once he does maybe we'll have more answers."

"And Justin? Have you heard from him?"

He shook his head, his rich, dark hair gleaming in the artificial light. "Not a word."

"Doesn't that worry you?"

A small, humorless smile lifted the corners of his mouth. "Everything Justin has done since the age of about ten has made me worried."

"Sounds like me and my sister."

"She a handful?" he asked.

"Definitely." Grace frowned as she thought of her younger sister.

"How did your parents deal with her?" He picked up his drink and took a sip, then returned the glass to the end table.

"They didn't. I mean, Natalie and I never knew our fathers. My mother was an unusual woman. She never wanted a man in her life on a permanent basis." Grace felt herself begin to relax, grateful to talk about anything except what had happened earlier that day.

"I'm not sure why she had Natalie. I'm not even sure why she had me. She certainly wasn't mother material. She was wealthy and beautiful. She was also cold and distant and loved to travel. By the age of six I pretty well knew I was on my own. When Natalie came along I was the one who raised her, and I think sometimes I was way too indulgent with her."

"Welcome to my club," he replied drily. "Only in our case it wasn't a problem of a cold and distant mother, it was an issue of a tough, tyrannical father who thought a beating a day made a better kid. It didn't take long when we were kids to realize that most of his rage for some unknown reason seemed to be directed at Justin. Of course, Justin was good at stirring up trouble."

"What about Jeffrey?"

Jake flashed her a smile that warmed every cold spot her body might have held. "The middle child. He was good at being invisible, especially when Dad was in one of his rages."

"And what about you?" she asked. She told herself that her interest was only in learning more about the family where her children's father came from and nothing personal as far as Jake was concerned.

"What about me? I got through it just like Jeffrey and Justin did. I was tougher than them, tried to protect them when I could. My mother died a year before my father. She got sick, and I think she just died to get away from him. But we all survived and here we are."

Grace had a feeling there were plenty of scars beneath the surface in all of the Johnson men. She couldn't help remembering Kerri saying that Jake was the alpha dog. She wondered how many beatings he'd taken on behalf of his brothers.

She'd certainly had more than her share

of sleepless nights where Natalie was concerned. There were times Grace wondered if Natalie was doing drugs and hanging out with the wrong kind of people. Grace tried to be a good sister, a good mentor, but there was no question that since their mother's death the relationship between the two sisters had gotten worse instead of better.

"So, what do you do in your spare time, Grace?" He smiled ruefully. "I mean, before the babies came when you had spare time."

"Nothing very exciting," she replied, grateful for the change in subject. "I enjoy cooking and food. I used to really enjoy going out to dinner, trying new restaurants and food experiences. I like to read and go to the movies. My life was fairly quiet before the girls came along. What about you? What do you like to do?"

"Enjoying good food is right up there at the top." He seemed to be relaxing also. Some of the tension that had been in his body language disappeared and the stern lines along the sides of his handsome face relaxed. "But I'm definitely happiest on the back of a horse riding the pastures and dealing with the ranch. You ride?"

"I took riding lessons when I was younger. It was one of those wild hairs my mother got. She decided her daughter should know how to ride. The lessons lasted about four weeks and then she had me quit and take tennis classes. But I enjoyed riding for the brief time I got to try it."

"I guess having the triplets changed your life considerably."

She laughed. "That's the understatement of the year. I've definitely had to sacrifice some things, but any sacrifice has been worth it. I've never known the kind of joy and love they've each brought into my life."

She sobered and met his gaze seriously. The conversation had been going too light and easy. She almost hated to mention his brother's name again, but she wanted Jake to understand exactly where she was coming from.

"I'll be fine without Justin. We'll all be fine without him. When my mother died she left both me and my sister a bit of an inheritance and then left the bulk of her estate to the triplets, so I'll never have to worry about college funds or buying cars or any kind of financial burden where they're concerned. I just didn't want them to grow up without a father like I had to. Little girls need daddies."

The tension lines were back in Jake's face as he reached for his drink once again. "I

can't make him be what you need him to be."
There was genuine pain in his voice.

"I know. I just want you to know that whatever happens I appreciate the hospitality you
and Kerri and Jeffrey have given us here."

"You're welcome. And you should have
your sling on," he said with a touch of cen-
sure in his voice.

But it wasn't the tone of his voice that made
her feel the absence of the cumbersome sling,
rather it was the quick slide of his dark gaze
down the length of her body that suddenly
made her feel half-naked.

Tension crackled in her head, in the very
air between them, and Grace recognized it
for what it was—a sexual awareness, a heady
whisper of desire she hadn't felt for any man
in a very long time.

Just that quickly it felt more than a bit dangerous to her, to sit here in the middle of the night with him, to be exchanging bits and pieces of their personal lives with each other. She was all too aware of her lack of clothing, and her body felt fevered despite the light-weight nightgown and robe that she wore.

She wondered what it would be like to kiss him. His mouth would taste of the Scotch he'd been drinking, and she knew the kiss would be heady and hot. She had a feeling he'd kiss with the same intensity he did everything else, that it would be an experience difficult for a woman to ever forget.

His cell phone rang, shattering the uncom-fortable silence that had sprung up between them and the risky direction of her thoughts.

He pulled his cell phone from his pocket and answered. A deep frown slashed across his forehead as he listened to whoever was on the other end of the line. "Yeah, okay. I'll be right there." He closed the phone and dropped it back in his pocket with a weary sigh.

"My brother has finally put in an appearance. He and a couple of his no-account friends showed up at Tony's Tavern, a bar in town. They were all drunk and disorderly and Sheriff Hicks is holding them at the jail." He got up from his chair and she rose from the sofa. "You should probably get some sleep. I'm sure I'll have some news about Justin first thing in the morning."

She walked with him to the bottom of the stairs. She felt the need to say something, anything to ease the worry lines on his face, to rid him of some of the tension that held his shoulders so rigid. But what could she say?

It was possible Justin and his friends were the ones who had gotten drunk and shot at her. It was also possible Justin had spent the afternoon getting drunk with his friends and had been nowhere around when the shooting had occurred.

In either case it was obvious Jake had his hands full with the brother he obviously loved, and Grace could relate to that because of her often difficult relationship and worries about Natalie.

"I'll see you in the morning," he said. Once again his gaze slid down, lingering briefly on the exposed skin of her collarbone, the curve of her breasts beneath the silk material. "Good night, Grace."

"Good night, Jake."

As he went out the front door she began to climb the stairs, the heat of his gaze still warming her stomach.

How was this even possible? How could she

be so attracted to Jake? The answer wasn't so complex—because he was hot and stable, because he'd been kind to her and seemed to be everything opposite of the man who'd already let her down. More important, because when his gaze had slid over her she'd sensed with a woman's instinct that he definitely felt something for her, too.

Once her shoulder was well enough she would leave here and probably never see any of the Johnson triplets again. One of them had already let her down and might have been responsible for trying to shoot her, and she'd be a fool to allow another of the hot, handsome triplets to get close to her in any way.

Jake gripped the steering wheel tightly as he headed toward Cameron Creek and the sheriff's office, which had become far too familiar in the past couple of years.

What he didn't want to think about was Grace in that sexy robe that had wrapped around her slender body just tight enough to display all the curves she possessed—and she possessed plenty.

He liked her. It wasn't just the way she looked in her sexy black-and-red robe with her hair slightly tousled. He liked the warmth of her smile, the way she loved her children. He liked the strength she obviously possessed, a strength that had seen her through a rough childhood and had buoyed her up as she'd become caretaker for a younger, obviously troubled sister.

She'd have to be strong to get through what had probably been a difficult pregnancy and the first ten months of raising those girls all alone.

If that wasn't enough, the smoky green of her eyes drew him in, the whisper of her perfume muddied his senses, and yet the very last thing he wanted in his own life was a woman and three children. Justin's problem, he reminded himself.

He just needed to get Justin home and sobered up and find out if he had anything to do with the attack on Grace that afternoon. There was nothing that would make him believe that Justin had been a part of the shooting unless he heard those words from his brother's own mouth.

Justin was thoughtless, irresponsible and showed poor judgment most of the time, but he wasn't a mean man. He didn't have the cruel streak that their father had exhibited over the years.

If any of them had that capacity it was Jake at this moment, who would like nothing better than to wrap his hands around his brother's throat and squeeze a little bit of sense into him.

Grace and the babies might go back to Wichita, but that didn't mean they just went away. Somehow, someday, Justin was going to have to face his daughters. He could do it now with love and support or he would do it later met with bitterness and recriminations from three young women who would have hard questions about where he'd been all their lives.

Jake desperately wanted his brother to make the right choice now and save those little girls a lot of heartache and tears down the road.

The sheriff's station was located on Main Street. It was a small, unassuming brick building with a couple of jail cells that were rarely used in the basement.

For a moment Jake remained in his car, staring at the building where he'd spent far too much of his time lately. Justin liked to drink, and when he drank he got stupid.

Jake had bailed him out of jail or talked Sheriff Hicks into just letting Justin go more times than he could count, and here he was again, riding to the rescue. Wearily he got out of the car and headed for the front door.

Lindsay Sanders sat at the front desk and gave him a rueful smile as he walked in. "We've got to stop meeting like this," she said, a slightly flirtatious glint in her dark eyes.

Jake didn't bite. He never did. "Hicks in his office?" he asked.

She nodded, as usual a hint of disappointment in her eyes as he refused to flirt with her. "He's waiting for you."

As Jake walked down the hallway to the sheriff's inner office, he thought of Lindsay. She was an attractive single woman who more than once had let him know she was available.

Maybe he should bite, he thought. Then he realized the only reason the idea had crossed his mind was because he thought it might get the scent of Grace out of his head, the memory of how she'd felt in his arms out of his brain.

He gave one short rap on Sheriff Hicks's door and then opened it, catching the older man with his feet up on his desk, his chair reclined and his hat over his eyes.

"I should be home in bed with my wife,"

he said without moving. "I should be dreaming about a native woman named Lola feeding me fresh mango on an exotic island." He pulled his feet off the desk, shoved his hat to the top of his head and sat up. "You know I'm only still here because it's you."

"I know, and I appreciate it," Jake said. He sank down in the chair opposite the desk. "Did he tell you where he was at the time of the shooting out at my place?"

Hicks snorted. "He told me that, along with intimate details of his relationship with Shirley and every other woman he's dated, and some crude jokes that made his two friends laugh like the drunken hyenas they are. He told me that he and Shirley had fought earlier this morning and he'd dropped her off at her place, then he hightailed it over to Elliot Spencer's house, they called J. D. Richards to join them there and they proceeded to get trashed. Elliot's wife confirmed that the three were there all day until they left late this evening."

"So he couldn't have been at my place firing shots at Grace." Jake hadn't realized how tight the knot had been in his chest until this moment when it eased somewhat.

"If you're to believe the two drunks that are with him and Elliot's wife—and I've got no reason not to believe Darla. She never lies to cover for her husband. According to them, they were all at Elliot's place until about an hour ago when they thought it was a good idea to show up at Tony's. The bartender called me, said they were out of their minds drunk and he was afraid there might be trouble. So I rounded them up and brought them here more for their own safekeeping than anything else."

Greg reared back in his chair. "It appears J.D. and Elliot will be my guests and sleep it off for the duration of the night. J.D. has nobody who is willing to come and get him and Darla told me to keep Elliot until he's sober. I'm assuming you're here to take Justin home."

"Unless there's some charges pending?"

Greg shook his head. "Fortunately for them I can't charge for stupidity, otherwise none of them would ever get out of here."

"Anything new on the drifter?" Jake asked.

"Nothing, but I've got my men still looking for him. I'll keep you posted." He got out of his chair and Jake stood as well. He knew the routine. Together he and Greg would take the stairs down to the bottom floor where Greg would unlock the cell door and Justin would stagger out.

It had been a long time since Jake had felt any kind of embarrassment over this situation. Weary resignation was what sat heavily on his shoulders as he followed Greg down the stairs that led to the cells.

And if the current situation wasn't tough enough, he had to face the fact that tomorrow Jeffrey and Kerri were leaving and that meant he'd be responsible for helping Grace with the three girls.

Not going to happen, he determined. One way or the other he was going to sober up his brother and force him to take some responsibility, at least until Jeffrey and Kerri got back into town or Grace healed up enough to take her girls and head home.

The cell area smelled like a brewery. J.D.

was on his back, snoring loud enough to wake the dead, and Elliot sat on the edge of the bunk, staring off into space in an obvious drunken stupor. Only Justin was animated, staggering back and forth in front of the bars and muttering beneath his breath.

"Hey!" His face lit at the sight of Jake. "There's my brother. He's the man. I knew he'd show up to get me out of here." He stepped back from the bars so Sheriff Hicks could unlock the door.

Justin stumbled out of the cell and threw an arm around Jake's shoulder, the smell of booze seeming to seep out of his very pores. "You know I love you, man."

"I know. Let's just get you home," Jake replied.

He got Justin loaded into his car and then headed to his brother's apartment. There were a million things Jake wanted to say to Justin, but he'd learned a long time ago not to argue or try to have a rational discussion with a drunk.

Within minutes Justin had fallen sound asleep. By the time Jake arrived at the apartment building he had to help his brother out of the car and into his place.

Justin went directly to the bedroom and fell onto the bed, passed out cold. Jake remained standing just inside the door of the one-bedroom apartment looking around in dismay.

Pizza boxes and food wrappers littered the floor, along with beer bottles and other trash items. The place looked like a room after a frat party had taken place, but Justin was no college kid. He was a thirty-five-year-old father of three and somehow, some way, Jake had to figure out how to make him step up to be a man.

Jake cleared a space on the sofa and sank down. He'd wait for Justin to sleep it off and then he and his brother were going to have a man-to-man talk that would get Jake out of the middle of this mess and away from the woman and the little girls he feared had the potential to make him rethink his desire to spend his life alone. And that would be the biggest mistake he'd ever make in his life.

Chapter 6

"You and Jeffrey are leaving today?" Grace stared at Kerri in stunned surprise.

"We'll only be gone for three nights," Kerri said as she refilled Grace's cup of coffee. "It's kind of our honeymoon/anniversary trip. When we got married we never took a honeymoon. We both agreed that for our first anniversary we'd stay at The Bouquet Bed and Breakfast in Topeka. But it's a really popular place and we had to book almost a year in advance."

Kerri rejoined Grace at the table. "If you're worried how you'll do without us, you shouldn't. Jake will take good care of you and the girls. He's perfectly capable of changing diapers and doing whatever else is necessary for you to get along just fine."

"It seems as though Jake takes care of everything and everyone," Grace replied. There had been no sign of Jake since he'd left the night before to retrieve Justin from the sheriff's office. "I imagine the last thing he'll want to do is spend the next couple of days taking care of me and the girls." Worry worked through her, along with a sense of dread at the thought of it just being her and Jake alone.

She told herself she was worried about how the two of them would deal with the responsibilities of the girls, but it was more than that.

Some of her worry had to do with that slow slide of his gaze down her body and the responding heat she'd felt whenever he looked at her.

"Jake always steps up to do the right thing. Don't you worry. Now, if you don't mind I'm going to excuse myself and tend to some packing."

As Kerri disappeared from the kitchen, Grace fought back a wild sense of panic. If she could heal her shoulder through sheer willpower alone, she would have done it at that very moment sitting at his kitchen table. She looked at the girls playing on the floor and frowned. Her shoulder was still sore enough that she couldn't even pick up one of her daughters.

She'd tried to call Natalie twice that morning to see if perhaps she could somehow get a ride here and take Grace home and then stay with her or help her find a nurse to hire until Grace's shoulder was healed enough for her to be on her own.

Unfortunately, Natalie hadn't answered her phone, and knowing her sister she was probably still in bed despite the fact that it was after ten.

Maybe by tomorrow she'd be well enough to go home, she thought. She experimentally moved her shoulder and gasped at the pain that sliced through her. Okay, maybe not tomorrow, but perhaps the next day she told herself. As soon as possible, that's all she could promise.

She finished her coffee and carried the cup to the sink. Once she'd rinsed it and placed it in the dishwasher, she decided she'd rather sit in the living room than in the kitchen, which required her moving the girls. She was trying to figure out how to make the transition when Jake and Justin walked in.

Jake looked grim and determined and Justin looked hungover and contrite. "Hey, Grace," Justin said, but it was the sight of Jake that made Grace's heart beat a little faster.

"I think it's time we all sit down and have some sort of a rational talk," Jake said.

"I was just going to move into the living room," she replied and looked pointedly at the girls. "If somebody will hand me one of them, I can manage one if you can get the other two."

Jake picked up Casey and landed her on Grace's hip on her good side. Then he picked up Bonnie, who snuggled into him with a contented grunt. Justin looked at the last triplet. "Who is that one?" he asked.

"That's Abby, and she doesn't have enough teeth to bite hard," Grace said drily.

Justin paused a moment as if unsure what to do, then he finally picked her up and Abby immediately began to fuss. "Why don't we go ahead and take them upstairs," Grace said as she changed her mind. "They're probably ready for a nap and it will be much easier for all of us to talk if it's just the adults." Although in Justin's case, she thought, she used the term "adult" very loosely.

Minutes later with the girls in their cribs, the three adults returned to the living room. Jake sat next to Grace on the sofa and Justin sat in the chair facing them, still looking slightly green around the gills.

"Look, the first thing I want to do is get something straight. I had nothing to do with the shooting that happened here," Justin said.

"I swear I left here and took Shirley home and then went directly to Elliot's where I spent the whole day." He leaned forward, his features pale but earnest as he looked at her. "Grace, I'd never do anything like that. I'd never want to hurt you. Heck, I'd never try to hurt anyone."

Grace wanted to believe him. No matter what their relationship, no matter what she thought of him personally, he was the father of her children.

Justin shot a glance at his brother and then looked back at Grace. "I don't know what happened or who took those shots at you, but I had absolutely nothing to do with any of it." He leaned back in his chair and ran a hand across his forehead, as if he had a hangover headache. "So, where do we go from here?"

"I'd say that's pretty much up to you," she

replied, not feeling a bit sorry for him. There was a little wicked part of her that hoped his hangover lasted for at least another twenty-four hours. "I mean, right now I'm here, the girls are here, but I've been trying to get in touch with my sister to see if maybe she can come and take me back to Wichita."

"You aren't in any condition to go home," Jake protested.

"I figured I could hire a nurse to help me for a couple of days," she explained. "With Jeffrey and Kerri leaving town, perhaps that would be best for everyone."

"That's not necessary," Jake replied smoothly. "You should be fine in a couple of days, and I'm sure between the three of us we can manage to take care of things here until you're healed up enough to go back home."

Grace thought Justin's face blanched

slightly at the prospect of being part of the team for the next few days; but there was such a ring of certainty in Jake's voice she almost believed that it would be okay.

Besides, no matter how much Grace told herself that Natalie would step up if necessary, she knew from experience her sister was nobody to count on. In that respect she and Jake shared a lot in common.

"I know I've acted badly so far," Justin said to her. "And I want to do the right thing, I really do. I'm just not sure what you expect from me. I mean, I've never been in this position before."

Just love my babies, love your daughters, she thought. It was that easy as far as she was concerned. It was all she really wanted or needed from him. "The first thing I'd like is just for you to get to know the girls while I'm here," she said aloud.

"I can do that," he agreed readily. "I still can't believe there's three of them, but I guess I shouldn't be surprised. I mean, with me being a triplet and all."

"I was definitely surprised when the doctor told me," Grace said drily. "I had no idea you were a triplet."

"Yeah, I guess I didn't mention that the night of the wedding."

Grace felt her cheeks warm. She didn't even want to think about that crazy night. There was plenty they hadn't talked about. "And then before I leave here maybe we could work out some sort of visitation for once I go back to Wichita," she said.

She wanted so much more than that. She wanted him not just to be a father who occasionally saw his girls on a weekend here and there, but rather she wanted him to be a dad in every loving sense of the word.

"That sounds good," Justin said agreeably and flashed another quick look at Jake. "So, maybe I should go home and pack a suitcase and plan on moving in here while Kerri and Jeffrey are gone." He looked at his watch. "I should be able to pack up and be back by the time the girls wake up from their naps."

"I think that sounds like a perfect idea," Jake said. Grace was sure he was more than a little bit eager to get out of the middle of this whole mess.

He'd been thrust into this drama through no fault of his own. He'd already told her he had no interest in having a wife or a family, and yet she was sure he'd felt saddled with the weight of her and the triplets for the last couple of days. And unless Justin stepped up, nothing was going to change in the immediate future.

Justin shot out of his chair. "Then I'll be back here in about an hour or so." He flashed them both a boyish smile as he flew out the front door.

"Do you really think we'll see him again today?" Grace asked Jake after Justin had disappeared.

"Who knows? I can only hope he'll do the right thing."

She offered him a tentative smile. "That's the way I feel about my sister. I've given up trying to force her to make the right choices and just spend a lot of time hoping she'll eventually grow up."

"In any case, we'll figure things out, and you don't need to worry about Kerri and

Jeffrey leaving. Surely if it comes to that, between the two of us we can easily handle three little girls."

Three hours later she had a feeling Jake was eating those very words. Kerri and Jeffrey had left for their trip an hour earlier, Justin had never returned and at the moment Jake was on the floor covered with babies.

Bonnie bounced up and down on his chest, Abby had him by the hair and Casey crawled back and forth over his legs as if they were the most fascinating obstacle course she'd ever encountered.

The whole thing had begun with a diaper change that had quickly spiraled out of control as the triplets saw Jake on the floor as a brand-new fun toy.

For the first time in days Grace's laughter bubbled out of her as Jake wrestled with the girls, and his laughter and their giggles combined to make sweet music to her ears.

He seemed surprisingly at ease with them considering how he'd acted the first time he'd been around them. He tweaked Bonnie's nose and tickled Abby's belly and then reached to tousle Casey's hair as they all laughed.

"Do they always have this much energy?" he asked as he finally managed to extricate himself and get to his feet.

"Mostly in the afternoons right after their naps," she replied. She thought he'd never looked as sexy as he did now with his dark rich hair mussed, a stain that looked suspiciously like drool on the front of his shirt and a genuine smile of amusement lifting the corners of his mouth.

This was a side of Jake she hadn't seen before, and it was breathtakingly appealing.

Fun-loving and with laughter lighting his eyes, he made a wistful want rise up inside of her. There was a little part of her that warned her not to get caught up in him, not to allow herself to like him so much.

It was at that moment she recognized that she'd arrived here with a little fantasy running in the back of her head—the fantasy that she'd come here, reunite with Justin and they would fall in love and get married and parent their children together and live happily ever after.

From the moment MysteryMom had given her this address, the image of a happily-ever-after had begun to form in her head. She hadn't consciously built it, but it had been there all the same.

That fantasy had been smashed into pieces the moment she'd had her first encounter with

Justin. She warned herself now that no good would come from her falling in love with Jake. It would just be plain stupid and too weird for them to get involved in any way. He was the wrong brother. It would only complicate what was already a complicated situation.

"How about dinner out tonight?" Jake asked an hour later. He felt the need to get them all out of the house that for the last hour had rung with Grace's laughter, with the giggles of the delightful little girls and with his own.

The girls had been all wiggling warmth as they'd crawled all over him. They'd smelled of baby fresh powder and everything innocent in the world.

God, he couldn't remember the last time he'd laughed with such abandon. It had felt so good, so right. It had been frightening. He'd had a momentary glimpse of what life might have been in this big house if he allowed himself a future that included others, if he allowed himself a future that included Grace and the girls.

"Oh, Jake, I'm not sure that's such a great idea. It's quite a job to get everyone ready and into a restaurant." Even as she said the words there was a faint wistfulness in her pretty eyes. "I haven't attempted to go out to eat since they were born."

"Then I'd say it's high time you did. Surely between the two of us we can manage it. There's a pretty good Italian restaurant in Cameron Creek. Actually, it's the only real restaurant in town, and I have a sudden hankering for some lasagna."

She ran a hand through her blond-streaked

brown hair and looked down at her jeans and T-shirt. Although he thought she looked lovely just the way she was, it was fairly easy to read her mind. "Why don't I keep an eye on the girls while you go do whatever it is women do before they go out to dinner?"

"Are you sure you really want to attempt this?" she asked hesitantly.

"Positive."

She smiled at him gratefully. The warmth of her smile coiled a ball of heat in the pit of his stomach. As she raced up the stairs, leaving him in the living room with the girls, he tried to control not just the physical desire she created inside him, but also a nebulous desire for something more.

Dinner out with the triplets would surely staunch any crazy feelings that were brewing inside him. There was no doubt in his mind that the evening would be utter chaos, just what he needed to remind himself of how much he didn't want this kind of chaos in his life.

When Grace came back down the stairs to go to dinner, all thoughts flew out of his head. She'd changed into a royal-blue dress that clung to her every curve and enhanced the lighter highlights of her hair. Her long legs looked silken and her feet were dainty in dark blue high-heel sandals whose open toes displayed pretty pink polish.

She looked elegant and sexy and nearly stole his breath away. "Wow, you clean up real nice," he finally managed to say.

Her cheeks grew pink and she ran a hand down the skirt. "Too much? I threw this into my suitcase last minute in case..." She allowed her voice to trail off as her blush darkened.

He knew what she'd been about to say— she'd packed the dress in case Justin decided to take her and the girls out someplace.

He shook his head. "Not at all. Very all right. I'll just go do a quick change myself and then we'll get this show on the road." He hurried upstairs to his own bedroom, trying to still the crazy beat of his heart.

Within a couple of weeks Jeffrey and Kerri would be moved out, Justin would still be living in his pigpen of an apartment and this big house would be all Jake's. It would resonate with the silence he'd longed for most of his life, and he'd be responsible for nothing more than his own happiness.

All he had to do was be patient, and in a short period of time Grace and the girls would be back to their lives and his brothers would be living theirs elsewhere. Then it would finally be his turn to truly be alone. He had to hang on to that thought, had to remember that it was his dream for himself.

He changed into a pair of dress slacks and a clean shirt, slapped a little cologne on the underside of his jaw and went back downstairs.

"Do you ever dress them all alike?" he asked when he rejoined her in the living room.

"Never. I figure when they're older if they want to dress alike that will be their choice, but I thought it was important at the very beginning that they each have their own identities. Did your parents dress you all alike?"

"Blue jeans and white T-shirts were our uniform for most of our childhood," he replied. "Mom and Dad never had any trouble telling us apart. Now, let's get on the road."

It took nearly thirty minutes to load up all the car seats and diaper bags and get the girls buckled in safely in the backseat of Jake's car. It would have been easier to take her car, but Jake insisted they take his. He hadn't forgotten that somebody had shot at her. He thought it safer to be in his vehicle.

"And that's why I don't go out," Grace said once they were finally settled in the car and headed down the road.

"It is a big job, isn't it?"

"Especially for one person. Usually by the time I get them all loaded up and ready to go, I've forgotten where I intended to go in the first place," she said with a smile.

"And your sister isn't a lot of help?"

"My sister helps when it's convenient for

her, which is very rare. Lately she's been far too busy with a new boyfriend to have much time for me."

"Nice guy?" He tried not to notice that scent of her, the fragrance that seemed to reach inside him and stir up all kinds of crazy desires.

"She says so, but I haven't met him yet, which worries me a little bit. If past behavior dictates future behavior, then he's probably a loser and a user. She doesn't have a terrific track record when it comes to men." Grace released a self-deprecating laugh. "Of course, I should talk." She frowned suddenly. "Sorry, I shouldn't have said that."

"Let's make a deal that we won't talk about Justin for the rest of the night. To be honest, I've had about all the drama I can take where my brother is concerned right now."

"It's a deal," she replied easily.

In the backseat, the little girls gibbered to each other, creating a pleasant white noise that filled the silence that suddenly grew between him and Grace.

"Do you think they know what they're saying to each other?" he asked.

"Who knows? They say twins sometimes develop a language of their own. They certainly spend a lot of time gabbing to one another."

"Probably discussing how foolish adults can be," he said drily, and was rewarded with one of her warm, beautiful laughs.

"They do laugh a lot," she replied.

It didn't take long for them to arrive at Maria's, the only Italian restaurant the small town of Cameron Creek boasted. In fact, it was the only official restaurant in town, although there was a fast-food place, a pizza parlor and a small café, as well.

It took much longer for them to finally get settled at a table with three high chairs the waitstaff had hurried to round up and provide. The triplets garnered plenty of attention from the other diners, but just as quickly the novelty wore off and people got back to focusing on their own meals.

Once the girls were happily settled with sippy cups and crackers and Jake and Grace had ordered their dinners and both had a glass of wine in front of them, Jake leaned back in his chair and began to relax for the first time in days.

"Tell me more about your mother," he asked, wanting to talk about anything but his own family. He also wanted to focus on something other than how the blue of Grace's dress contrasted with the beautiful green of her eyes, how the scoop neckline gave him just a glimpse of the top of her creamy breasts.

"She was a very successful interior designer. She owned her own company and had famous clients on both coasts. She went on buying trips all the time to Paris and Italy, and I think I was probably one of the few things she acquired that was disappointing."

"What makes you say that?" he asked in surprise.

"Mother wanted a mini-me and I was absolutely nothing like her. I didn't care about what a chair cost or where it came from. I didn't appreciate expensive clothes or shoes or any of the finer things in life. I loved animals and children and knew I wanted to be a teacher when I was still in grade school."

"An admirable profession," he commented.

Her hair looked like spun silk in the candle-light that flickered in the center of their table. More than anything he wanted to reach his hand out and touch it, wrap one of the loose curls around his fingers and draw her closer to him.

At that moment Bonnie banged her sippy cup on her high chair tray. "More," she said and pointed to the box of crackers visible in the diaper bag.

Without missing a beat Grace gave each of the girls another cracker. "Natalie was much more like my mother. She loves nice things and she was desperate for my mother's attention. Sometimes she got it and sometimes she didn't." She paused to take a sip of her wine. "Sometimes I think I've indulged her too much to try to make up for the attention she didn't get from our mother. And without any father present in her life, I think it was really difficult for her."

"Family dynamics can definitely be difficult," he replied. "Even though my brothers are the same age as me, I feel as if I've been taking care of them all my life. That's why I've decided never to marry or have kids of my own. Once Kerri and Jeffrey move out I'm looking forward to being alone for the rest of my life with nobody to take care of ever again."

She smiled ruefully. "And here I am with a busted-up shoulder and three babies depending on you for the time being."

"But it's not permanent," he countered. "Although, no matter what happens with you and Justin, I'll always consider you and the girls a part of the family." He could tell his words touched her.

"That's nice, but we both know how this is going to work. I'm going to leave here and probably never see or hear from Justin again. I'll get on with my life and you all will get on with yours. The odds of us staying in touch are pretty minimal." There was no self-pity or recrimination in her voice, just a calm stating of the facts of reality.

At that moment the waitress arrived with their orders. "They may need to get out the garden hose after we're finished here," Grace said with a touch of humor as she scooped up a small serving of spaghetti on three little plates for the triplets.

Jake had expected chaos, and there was, but there was also a lot of laughter as they ate the meal. Casey picked at her spaghetti with dainty fingers and ate one noodle at a time. Abby seemed more interested in the people around them than in the food in front of her. But Bonnie ate with gusto, smooshing the spaghetti into her mouth until sauce decorated her face from ear to ear.

As the kids ate, Grace and Jake enjoyed their meals, but even more, Jake enjoyed the conversation. He liked the way her eyes sparkled as she talked about teaching, sharing funny stories of the children who had passed through her classes. It was obvious that she was well suited to be a teacher, not only from her love of children, but also by the steady patience he sensed in her.

All the qualities that made her a good teacher made her a great mother. Her patience throughout the meal with the girls never wavered, not with spilled drinks, sloppy faces and an occasional cry for attention.

She was beautiful and quick-witted, and

every minute he spent with her fed a well of desire that he knew was dangerous. He wanted her. He wanted her in his bed, but the last thing she needed was another Johnson man to take advantage of her and let her down.

And he would let her down. Just like his brother, Jake had no interest in being a husband or a parent for her or any other woman. Still, that didn't mean he didn't enjoy the here and now with her and the girls. And it didn't mean he wouldn't enjoy having her in his bed for just a single night.

When he'd offered dinner out he'd expected a frantic chaos that would turn him off, but instead what he'd found was three well-behaved little girls and a delightful dinner companion who stirred all the senses he possessed.

When they were finished eating, Grace cleaned off the girls' faces and hands with wet wipes and then looked at him. "Do you mind holding down the fort for a few minutes while I make a fast trip to the ladies' room?"

"We'll be fine," he agreed with a smile to the shiny clean faces of the triplets. "While you're gone I'll settle up the bill." He raised a hand as she started to protest. "My idea, my treat."

"Thank you," she said graciously.

He watched as she made her way to the back of the restaurant where the restrooms were located. Her hips held a subtle sway as she walked that enticed him more than a stripper's strut.

There was no cheap flash to Grace, just an understated sexuality coupled with a quiet elegance that made him wonder why Justin had pursued her in the first place.

Justin liked flash and Grace wasn't flashy. She was much more Jake's type. He clenched his jaw tight at this thought. Of course she wasn't his type. He didn't have a type. Hell, he didn't *want* a type.

At that moment, as if conjured up by his very thoughts alone, his brother entered the restaurant. Shirley was at his side, clinging to his arm like a tick to a big-haired dog.

Justin waved and wove through the tables toward Jake, who felt a rise of his blood pressure as they drew closer. This could not be good.

"Hey, what a coincidence seeing you here," Justin said with a bit of a sheepish grin.

"The way I remember our last conversation,

I was supposed to see you back at the house," Jake replied with a curt nod to Shirley.

"Yeah, but he forgot he had promised me dinner out tonight," Shirley exclaimed as she looked at the three little girls. "So, this is Moe, Larry and Curly?" she said.

Justin's laugh was cut short by Jake's glare.

"We were just getting ready to leave," Jake said. This had disaster written all over it, and he suddenly wanted to bundle up the girls and get them out of here and away from Shirley and Justin as quickly as possible.

Shirley glanced around and then smiled at Justin. "I'll be right back. I think I need to use the little girls' room."

Before Jake could stop her she took off in the direction Grace had just headed.

Chapter 7

It had been a wonderful night, and Grace couldn't remember the last time she'd enjoyed a man's company as much as she enjoyed Jake's. He scared her just a little bit—because she did like him so much, and because she knew there was nothing there for her or her daughters where he was concerned.

Still, it was far too easy to imagine herself and the girls living with Jake in that big house, sharing days filled with laughter and then going to sleep each night in the safety of his strong arms.

She shook her head to dispel the inappropriate visions. She'd be crazy to even entertain those kinds of dreams. That was definitely the stuff of heartbreak.

She was at the sink in the ladies' room washing her hands when the door opened and a tall blonde woman walked in. She instantly recognized her as the woman who had been with Justin.

"Grace, we haven't officially met yet," the woman said. "My name is Shirley Caldwell. I'm Justin's fiancée, and I just wanted to let you know that you can't have him." She raised her chin in obvious defiance.

Grace fought the impulse to laugh. "That's fine, because I don't want him." She dried her hands and tossed the paper towel into the trash. "And I hope the two of you will be very happy together."

Shirley frowned, as if she was spoiling for a fight that she now recognized probably wasn't going to happen. "I'm going to give him lots of babies, and he'll never love yours like he'll love mine."

Grace saw the desperation in Shirley's eyes, heard it vibrating in her voice. This woman was obviously in love with Justin and saw Grace and the triplets as a threat to that love.

"Shirley, I'm not your enemy," she said as kindly as possible. "I don't want to take anything away from you and whatever life you build with Justin." She edged toward the door, just wanting to escape the awkward situation.

"We weren't together, you know, when you got pregnant. We weren't dating then so he didn't cheat on me to be with you." Shirley raised her chin proudly. "We've been together for six months and he loves me like he's never loved any woman before."

"Then I wish you both the best of luck." Grace left the bathroom with Shirley at her heels. She felt sorry for the woman, had a feeling there was plenty of heartache in her future if she was planning on hitching her star to Justin. She didn't even want to think about the fact that if Justin married Shirley, then Shirley would be the triplets' stepmother. That was the stuff of nightmares.

She was conscious of Shirley following right at her heels as she headed back to the table where Jake stood, a look of strain on his face, quickly followed by an expression of relief at the sight of her.

He stepped toward her and grabbed her

good arm. "You okay?" he asked with a quick glance at Shirley.

"I'm fine," she assured him, surprised by how much she liked the feel of his arm on hers. She felt protected by his nearness even though she didn't need any protection.

"Hi, Grace," Justin said. "Guess you and Shirley already met."

"We did," she replied, vaguely disappointed when Jake dropped his hand and stepped away from her.

"Good, then you can help me carry the girls out to the car," he said to his brother. He plucked Casey from her high chair and handed her to the surprised Justin. "As you can see, it's difficult for Grace to carry the kids with her arm in the sling. Shirley, if you can grab that diaper bag, then we can all get the girls settled into my car."

There was a ring of authority in Jake's voice that Grace was surprised both Justin and Shirley responded to. Jake picked up Abby and Bonnie, and Grace followed them all, slightly bemused by the procession that had her empty-handed and lagging behind.

"That has to be the most bizarre thing that has ever happened to me," she said moments later as Jake was driving her and the girls back to the ranch. "Starting with being confronted in the bathroom by my baby daddy's latest girlfriend."

Jake shot her a quick smile. "I was afraid I might have to storm in there to protect you from her pulling out all your hair or something."

"And what makes you think I couldn't have kicked the stuffing out of her if I'd needed to?" she countered with a grin.

"You look more like a lover than a fighter," he replied. He snapped his gaze from her to the street ahead and just that quickly it was there between them again, that simmering tension that curled heat in her stomach and made her want…something…something she shouldn't, something she couldn't have.

"It was a surprise to turn around from the sink in the bathroom and see Shirley standing there," she said in an effort to ease some of that tension. "She's in love with Justin. She just wanted to stake her claim."

"He'll only break her heart, too. That's what he does, breaks hearts."

Grace smiled. "He didn't break my heart. Oh, he might have destroyed a little fantasy I'd entertained."

Jake cast her a quick glance. "What kind of fantasy?"

"You know, the kind where I meet the man who fathered my children after a long time apart and sparks fly and we suddenly realize we belong together and live happily ever after."

"Did you really expect that to happen?"

"No, but as I was driving here I kind of hoped it might. Of course, it took about two seconds with Justin to realize that wasn't going to happen." She shifted her gaze and stared out the window into the darkness of the night. "But eventually I'll find my happily-ever-after, not just for my girls, but also for myself. I don't want to live alone like my mother did for all her life. I want somebody to share both the good times and the bad times with me. I want a soul mate."

"It's not going to be easy, finding a man who will not only want to be with you but will also want to be an instant father to three little girls."

"I know I'm a package deal. Nobody ever told me life would be easy," she replied. "It doesn't have to happen today or next week or even next year, but eventually I'll find a man who wants to be a part of my life and my children's lives."

"At this point I think we can both agree that it isn't going to be Justin," he said drily.

"We definitely can agree on that," she replied with a small laugh.

By this time they had reached the ranch, and all three of the girls had fallen sound asleep in their car seats.

Jake managed to place Casey over Grace's good shoulder and then he carried both Bonnie and Abby in his arms. He looked so right with a sleeping little girl in each arm as they climbed the stairs. He laid each of them in the crib with a gentleness that touched her heart.

He stepped to the back to the doorway as she covered each child and touched each sleeping face with love. Then, together, she and Jake went back down the stairs.

"How about some coffee?" he asked.

"Sounds good," she agreed. As she followed behind him toward the kitchen, she tried to tamp down the emotions that pressed tight in her chest where he was concerned.

Jake Johnson was getting to her, inching his way into her heart in a way that could only lead to heartbreak. She moved her shoulder beneath the sling, unsurprised by the sharp pain that was her reply.

Not yet. She wasn't ready to take off from here tomorrow, but maybe by the next day she could load up her daughters and head back home. In the meantime she just needed to guard her heart the best she could from Jake.

They lingered over coffee in the living room, continuing their conversation about everything and nothing. They talked about favorite foods and books read, about the antics of the girls and the fact that Bonnie would probably be the first of the three to walk.

"Abby is too content wherever she sits to walk too quickly. Casey is too shy to be the first one to explore the world of being upright. Bonnie is definitely my adventurous little soul," she said.

"She's a corker," he agreed with an easy smile.

"She definitely likes you."

"They all seem to like people," he replied.

"I think it's because from the time they

were two months old they've been in day care. They're used to seeing new people all the time."

Jake drained the last of the coffee from his cup. "We should probably go to bed. I imagine the girls are early risers."

"They are," she agreed, reluctant to call an end to what had been a wonderful evening. She stood and together she and Jake carried their coffee cups to the kitchen.

She wasn't sure exactly how it happened, but as they both reached to set their cups in the sink, her face was suddenly too close to his. His breath felt warm on her cheek and his eyes flared dark with a desire that was unmistakable.

They both straightened, and somewhere in the back of her mind she knew she should step away from him, gain some needed distance, but her feet refused to obey her mental command.

He was going to kiss her. She saw his intent shimmering in his eyes, and as sure as she knew he was going to kiss her she also knew she wasn't going to stop him.

She'd never wanted a kiss as much as she wanted his at this very moment. When he dipped his head she met him halfway, rising up on her tiptoes.

His mouth touched hers softly...tentatively at first, as if unsure of his own intent or his welcome. She opened her mouth and he took the welcome, deepening the kiss with a searing intensity that shot thrilling sensations through her body.

It lasted only a minute and then he stumbled back from her, his midnight-blue eyes still blazing with desire. "That was a mistake." His voice was deep, almost gravelly as his gaze lingered on her mouth.

"I agree." The words whispered from her with a sigh of longing.

"I want to do it again." The words sounded as if they'd been pulled from the very depths of him.

"Oh, Jake, I want you to."

The words were barely out of her mouth before his lips silenced her once again. Hot and greedy, his lips plied hers and she melted against him as well as her sling would allow.

His arms wound around her gently, as if he remembered her shoulder and didn't want to hurt her, yet needed her as close to him as possible. And she wanted to be that close.

His tongue swirled with hers, demanding a response that she gave eagerly. Somewhere in the back of her mind she knew this was wrong, so very wrong. This wasn't a man she should be kissing, this wasn't a man she should be wanting. But that didn't stop her from doing either.

His mouth finally left hers and trailed a blaze of hunger down the side of her throat. She dropped her head back with her eyes closed, dizzied by his scent and by his very touch.

He kissed her just behind one of her ears. "Stop," he murmured against the sensitive skin. "We have to stop this." He slowly dropped his arms from around her and once again stepped back, this time his eyes dark and unreadable. "I'm sorry. That shouldn't have happened."

"I know, but I wanted it as much as you did," she admitted, her voice slightly shaky with the emotions still raging through her. She still wanted him, she thought.

"You know by now that there's no future here with Justin. There's also no future for you here with me." He jammed his hands in his pockets, as if afraid of where they might wander if left somehow untethered.

"To be honest, I wasn't looking for any kind of a future. I was just in the moment and looking forward to the next. I'm a big girl, Jake, and you've made it very clear to me what your desire is about being alone for the rest of your life. I just thought maybe you didn't want to be alone tonight." She felt the burn of a blush fill her cheeks. She had never said anything so forward to a man before, but she'd also never felt this way about a man before.

The blaze was back in his eyes and she

wanted to fall into that dark fire and just for one night feel like a sexy woman, not like a schoolteacher with triplets. It was a foolish desire, but at the moment she wouldn't mind a little bit of foolishness with him.

"There's no question that there's something between us, Grace, some crazy physical attraction that has been there since the minute I laid eyes on you. But because we're adults we aren't going to follow through on it. It would only complicate what's already a pretty good mess."

She knew he was right. Now that the heat of the moment was passing, rational thought was returning. "I know you're right. You and I together would just be plain stupid. I just got carried away in the moment."

He offered her a small smile. "We both did. And now I think it's definitely time we say good-night." He didn't wait for her response but turned on his heels and left the kitchen.

Grace wasn't sure whether to be disappointed or glad at the way things had turned out. On the one hand, she knew that Jake would never be more than a one-night stand—the second in her life and another one with unwanted consequences. Although she wouldn't have wound up pregnant, she had a feeling it would have been impossible to keep her heart uninvolved.

On the other hand, she knew it would have been a night to remember when she was back home by herself and with that whisper of loneliness that sometimes struck her.

She turned off the kitchen light and then climbed the stairs and went directly into the room where the triplets were sleeping. She wanted to be the best possible mother she could be for them, but that didn't stop her needs and wants as a woman.

She'd told him the truth when she'd said she wanted somebody to share her life, a soul mate who would grow old with her and watch their grandchildren grow.

As she left the triplets' bedroom she glanced down the long hallway to the very end where she knew the master suite was located. Was Jake in bed now thinking about what might have happened? What could have happened if he hadn't stopped it?

Was he in bed still feeling the burn that filled her stomach, that ached deep inside her? She knew with a woman's certainty that if she walked down that hallway and opened the door to his bedroom they'd wind up in his bed making love.

Her feet actually took three steps in that direction before she stopped herself and instead turned and went into her own guest room.

At least this room didn't smell of his scent—that of a wonderfully clean male combined with a woodsy undertone. She'd cracked open the sliding door that led to the balcony earlier in the day and the slight breeze blowing through brought with it the scent of fresh grass, evening dew and country flowers.

She undressed and changed into her nightgown, then put the sling back on. She was going to try to sleep in it, although usually when she woke up in the mornings she discovered she'd taken it off at some point in the night.

As she placed her cell phone on the dresser, she realized she hadn't heard anything from Natalie that day. She wasn't sure if that was a good thing or bad.

Grace got into bed, feeling as if it had been a lifetime ago that she had loaded the girls into her car to leave Wichita. She'd had such hope in her heart that she'd come away from here with a father for the girls, a father who would love and emotionally support them as they flourished and grew.

She knew now that wasn't going to happen. If Justin wasn't the kind of stable, mature man he needed to be by the age of thirty-five, she didn't see it happening ever. She suspected Justin had a drinking problem, and that only added to the many reasons she knew he'd never be the man she wanted in her daughters' lives.

Maybe someday she would find somebody to love her, to love them, and he would take on the role of a good and loving stepfather.

Grace hoped if that ever happened it might be enough for the girls.

There was no way of knowing for sure, but her gut instinct told her that Justin hadn't had anything to do with whoever had shot at her. She was willing to believe the sheriff's speculation that a drifter had set up camp in the woods and in some deluded thinking had seen her walking around as a threat to his little temporary home.

Justin had been a mistake, and she was more than a little half-crazy for his brother. She squeezed her eyes closed, seeking sleep rather than thoughts of Jake.

Although her shoulder was still sore, it was less so than it had been. She was hoping that by the day after tomorrow at the very latest she could head home. She just needed to get back to her ordinary life, raising her children and enjoying the summer before fall came and she had to return to work.

With a deep sigh she closed her eyes, knowing she needed to get some sleep in order to have the energy to deal with her daughters and anything else that might come up the next day.

She wasn't sure what awakened her...a noise...a whisper of breath on the side of her face? For a sleepy, half-conscious moment she thought it was Jake who had come to her room to finish what they'd started earlier in the night.

She came fully awake and immediately a cloth was shoved in her mouth, preventing her from releasing the scream that instantly leapt to her lips.

Somebody jumped on top of her, although in the dark it was impossible to tell who it was. What was going on? She couldn't make sense of it. She only knew pure unadulterated terror as gloved hands wrapped around her neck and began to squeeze.

With one arm in her sling and her legs trapped beneath the sheets, she was nearly helpless in any effort to fight back. She flailed her good arm, trying to make contact with the face of the attacker.

Air.

She needed air.

Her lungs were slowly being depleted of precious oxygen as it was being squeezed from her. She bucked her hips, kicked wildly at the sheets and twisted her head back and forth, trying to break the grip on her throat.

Help! Somebody please help me!

The words screamed in her head but had no

way around whatever had been stuffed in her mouth as a gag. She was going to die!

Her babies. Who was going to take care of her babies? As she felt the edges of unconsciousness creeping in, she made one last desperate attempt to help herself. She flung her free arm out and it connected with the bedside lamp. The Tiffany-style light crashed to the floor with a shattering of glass and an answering cry came from one of the triplets.

Don't hurt my babies, she thought wildly.

The intruder jumped off Grace and ran for the balcony. As the person disappeared over the balcony edge, Grace pulled the gag from her mouth and released a scream.

Chapter 8

The crash awakened Jake from a wild, sexy dream about Grace. In the dream she'd been in his bed and they had been making love. The cry of one of the girls galvanized him to leave the dream behind, get out of bed and pull on his jeans. But the sound of Grace's scream shot him out of the room and down the hallway toward hers.

As he ran his heart pounded with adrenaline. What on earth would make her scream like that? He entered her room and flipped on the light to see her sitting up, her hand at her throat and utter terror shining wildly from her eyes.

By now all three girls were crying, but Jake's complete attention was focused on the woman in the bed. "What happened?" he asked, feeling as if his heart was about to pound out of his chest.

"Somebody came in…attacked me…he went over the balcony." The words rasped from her as she half stumbled from the bed. "I've got to get to the girls."

"Don't move," Jake replied. She looked as if she was in shock, her legs barely able to hold her up. Her throat was red and angry looking, and as Jake ran to the balcony there was nothing more he wanted to do than rip somebody's head off.

Unfortunately, as he stepped outside on the

balcony and looked around, there was nobody to see. The night was complete with darkness and barely a sliver of moonlight to faintly illuminate the landscape.

It was easy to tell how the intruder had gotten inside. The balcony could have been accessed by the sturdy wooden trellis that climbed up the house next to it, a trellis that would no longer exist after he got done with it.

He went back into the bedroom, closed and locked the sliding glass door, unsurprised to find Grace not there. Even crazy with fear and with her throat burning and raw, her first thought would be to soothe her crying daughters. He spied her cell phone on the dresser and used it to call Sheriff Hicks, then went to where he knew Grace would be.

Sure enough she was in the girls' bedroom,

moving from crib to crib in an effort to put the girls back to sleep, and it was working. As she rubbed a back, spoke softly and gave kisses, the girls eventually all settled back to sleep.

It was only when the room was quiet again that she met him in the hallway. He gestured for her to follow him back into the bedroom. There, under the overhead light, he could once again see the angry red ring that decorated her neck.

As he stared at it, she began to shiver, as if the initial shock was wearing off and now that she felt like her daughters didn't need her anymore she was about to fall to pieces.

He opened his arms and she collapsed against him, deep sobs ripping up from someplace deep inside her. He didn't ask any questions. Those would come later. For now he just held her as she trembled almost violently in his arms.

He would kill the person responsible for this. Anger roared through him as he held her tight, her heartbeat frantic against his own.

"Come on, let's go downstairs to wait for Greg," he finally said when some of the trembling had eased. He wanted to get her out of the bedroom where the attack had taken place in case there might be some evidence that could be collected.

"You called him?" she asked as she grabbed her robe. She pulled it around her and they left the bedroom.

"I did. He's on his way." He kept one arm around her as they went down the stairs and then he sat next to her on the sofa, still with an arm around her as she continued to shiver off and on.

"I had the sliding glass door open a little bit," she said, her voice filled with self-recrimination. "I didn't imagine that anyone could get inside. I didn't think that anyone would want to get inside, to get to me…to try to kill me." Her voice rose slightly with each word. "Why is this happening? Who's doing this to me?"

"Shh, it's all right now," Jake said, but his mind raced. This attack tonight put the shooting incident in a whole new light.

There was no mistaking the fact that somebody had breached the sanctity of his home in the middle of the night for the sole intent of hurting Grace. They'd climbed up that trellis, crept into her room and wrapped their hands around her throat.

That meant in all probability those shots had been intended specifically for Grace and not the result of some drifter trying to protect a temporary homestead.

Somebody had tried to kill Grace not once, but twice, and Jake had never felt so helpless or so damned angry in his entire life. Thankfully, at that moment Greg Hicks and a couple of his deputies showed up at the door.

Jake and Grace took the lawmen upstairs to the bedroom to explain what had happened. Two deputies stayed behind to begin collecting evidence and processing the scene while Greg, Jake and Grace returned to the living room so Greg could ask Grace some questions.

"Now, tell me exactly what happened," Greg said.

Jake was impressed by the way Grace had pulled herself together. The robe was belted tightly around her slender waist and she'd not only stopped trembling, but even had a steely strength radiating from her eyes.

"I woke up knowing somebody was in my room. Before I could do anything, he was on top of me and had shoved a gag into my mouth. Then he tried to strangle me."

She raised her hand to her neck. Some of the redness had faded, but the idea of anyone wrapping their hands around her neck, the throat he'd kissed with such desire earlier, filled Jake with new rage.

"I thought he was going to kill me. I tried to fight but with my sling on I only had one hand. I finally managed to knock over the lamp next to the bed, which woke up one of my girls, which apparently woke up Jake." She cast him a grateful look. "I pulled the gag out of my mouth and screamed."

"By the time I got to the bedroom, whoever had been inside was gone. I went out on the balcony but didn't see anyone. Unfortunately, there's no light out there so he could have been anywhere in the yard and I probably wouldn't have seen him."

"Do we know for sure it was a him?" Greg asked.

Grace looked at him in stunned surprise, as if the idea that her attacker might have been a woman hadn't occurred to her. It certainly hadn't occurred to Jake.

"I don't know," she said slowly. "I just assumed…" Once again her hand went to her throat. "The grip was awfully strong to be a woman. And the person felt heavy…big." She dropped her hand and released a deep sigh. "But I was also terrified out of my mind, and my perceptions of those moments could be way off."

"Hopefully Deputy Bartell and Deputy Lathrop will find something…a fingerprint or a hair," Greg replied.

Grace shook her head. "There won't be any fingerprints. Whoever it was, he or she was wearing gloves." She winced, as if able to feel those gloves still around her neck.

"Greg, you've got to do something about this," Jake snapped angrily, and then caught himself and offered a tight smile of apology. "Sorry, I didn't mean to yell at you. I'm just frustrated."

"Don't worry," Greg replied easily. "No offense taken."

"Does Shirley know how to fire a gun?" Grace asked. Both Greg and Jake looked at her in surprise. "Well, it's obvious she resents my connection to Justin. I was just wondering."

"I don't know if Shirley knows how to shoot

or not. Certainly most of the women around these parts aren't unfamiliar with guns," Greg replied. "I believe her daddy is a hunter."

Jake tried to wrap his mind around the idea of Shirley as some crazed, jealous killer. Crazed jealous girlfriend, yes, that was easy to imagine, but a killer? He'd known Shirley for most of his life and wouldn't have thought it of her, but wasn't this the kind of real-life stuff television movies were made of?

He listened as Grace explained to Greg about the earlier confrontation with Shirley in the ladies' room at the restaurant. "It wasn't really ugly," she said. "I assured her I had no grand design on Justin, and when Jake and I left them at the restaurant I assumed everything was fine between me and Shirley."

"So right now I've got a list with a grand total of two suspects on it—Justin and Shirley." Greg shook his head. "Justin's alibi for the time of the shooting was fairly solid. Maybe I need to have a little chat with Shirley about where she was when those shots were fired and where she was tonight. At least that's a place to start."

He looked at Grace for a long moment. "You sure there isn't somebody else in your life that might have a grudge against you?"

"A grudge deep enough to want me dead?" She gave a half-hysterical laugh. "Nobody that I can think of. I can't even imagine what Justin or Shirley would hope to gain by my death. None of this makes sense, none of it!"

Jake once again placed an arm around her shoulder as he heard the rising emotion in her voice. She was scared and bewildered and he felt the same way.

"I need to go home," she said, more to herself than to anyone in the room.

"I understand your desire, Ms. Sinclair, but I'd really like it if you'd stick around another couple of days while I do a little investigating," Greg said.

"I'll keep you safe, Grace," Jake exclaimed. "I'll turn this place into a damned fortress if necessary to make sure that nothing else happens to you while you and the girls are here."

She looked at Greg. "I'll stay through tomorrow, but first thing the next day I'm going back home."

Jake wanted to protest but realized he had no right to ask her to stay any longer. Justin had certainly given her no reason to hang around. Somebody had tried to kill her twice. Could he really blame her for wanting to get out of town as soon as possible?

He had a feeling if not for her shoulder injury she'd already be packed up and in her car headed back to Wichita. He knew with certainty that come hell or high water, she'd force her shoulder to be okay to get her out of here the day after tomorrow.

He should be glad to see her go. After all, that's what he'd wanted from the moment she'd shown up here with those adorable little girls and a gun in her pocket.

Thoughts of the gun sat him up straighter on the sofa. He hadn't thought about it since they'd locked it in his glove box at the hospital the day that Grace had fallen. If she'd had that gun tonight maybe she would have been able to stop the attack, wound the attacker. Or the gun could have been taken away from her and used on her instead.

A headache blossomed across his forehead,

along with a tight vise across his chest as he realized what might have happened tonight. If she hadn't managed to hit the lamp, if one of the girls hadn't started to cry, he might not have gotten out of bed and the intruder might have been successful in killing her.

Chapter 9

Grace awoke the next morning in Jake's king-size bed between the navy sheets that held his familiar scent. For a long moment she didn't move, just remained still and breathed in the essence of him.

After Greg and the deputies had finally left, Jake had insisted she sleep in here for what was left of the night while he bunked in Kerri and Jeffrey's room next door.

She'd expected to be awake all night. She'd expected to be scared senseless until dawn lit the morning skies. But almost the minute she'd wrapped herself in the sheets that smelled of Jake, she'd fallen into a deep, dreamless sleep.

She suddenly shot up, aware that the sun was drifting in through the window at an angle that let her know it was late. The girls! Why hadn't they awakened her with their morning cries? They never slept this late.

She jumped out of the bed and grabbed her robe and her cell phone from the nearby chair. She pulled on the robe as she raced out of the room and held the cell phone ready to call for help if necessary. She realized at some point in the night she must have taken her sling off in her sleep, but that didn't matter now. All that mattered was that she check on her daughters and make sure they were okay.

One glance in the girls' room showed three

empty cribs. Panic soared through Grace as she half ran, half stumbled down the stairs.

The normal scents of fresh-brewed coffee, crispy bacon and eggs calmed her as she entered the kitchen and saw her three girls all happily seated at their high chairs and enjoying a mess of scrambled eggs on their trays.

Jake stood at the stove with his back to her. He wore only a pair of jeans and was singing a rap-style rendition of "Rock-a-Bye Baby."

It was at that moment that Grace knew without a doubt that she was in love with him. She was head over heels in love with Jake Johnson.

She'd seen his tenderness with her daughters, tasted the passion in his kiss. She was in love with him and there was nothing she could do about it, no way to change it.

She must have made some sort of noise, for

he whirled around, spatula in hand, and gave her a smile that warmed her from her head to her toes.

"There she is, girls. Your mommy, our own sleeping beauty, has finally decided to get out of bed." He pointed her to a seat at the table. "Sit and relax. Bacon and eggs in about three minutes. I hope you like your eggs over however. Sometimes they're sunny and soft and sometimes they break."

"Over however is my very favorite," she said as she gave each girl a kiss on their foreheads, then sat at the table. Abby's T-shirt was on inside out and Bonnie was wearing Casey's shorts, but it was obvious Jake had done his best to get the girls up and dressed for the day.

She was grateful when he turned back to face the stove so she could have a moment to get her newly recognized emotion under control. She'd known she was getting too close to Jake, feeling wildly sexually attracted to him, but it wasn't until now that the full force of her love for him crashed inside her heart.

"Where's your sling?" he asked as he placed a plate of bacon, eggs and toast in front of her.

"Probably on the floor next to your bed. I take it off in my sleep. Aren't you eating?" she asked as she took the fork and napkin he offered her.

"Already ate. I wasn't sure what all the girls should have for breakfast so I smooshed up some banana for them before I gave them the eggs. Was that okay?"

"Perfect." His bare chest made it difficult for her to concentrate on anything he was saying. That muscled chest should be outlawed for its effect on helpless women trying to eat their breakfast.

He grabbed a cup of coffee and joined her at the table. "How did you sleep?"

"Surprisingly well, considering."

His eyes narrowed slightly and lingered on her throat. "How's your neck?"

"A little sore, but I'm going to be fine." She watched as he used a napkin and wiped egg from Casey's chin as if it was the most natural thing in the world for him to do.

"You'd make an awesome father, Jake." The words slipped from her unbidden.

He frowned and tossed the napkin aside. "I've spent most of my life fathering my brother. I don't have the desire or the energy to father anyone else."

"Why don't you stop?"

"Stop what?"

She broke off a piece of her toast, but instead of popping it into her mouth she set it on the side of her plate and kept her gaze focused on his eyes. "Why don't you stop fathering Justin?"

She could tell her question irritated him, and maybe that's what she'd intended. Maybe she wanted to see him a little bit angry with her to somehow diminish what was in her heart for him.

"It's complicated." He took a sip of his coffee and eyed her over the rim of the cup. When he lowered it he gave her a tight smile. "I could ask you the same question. Why are you still mothering your sister?"

She hadn't expected him to turn the tables on her. "Okay, you're right. It's complicated. There are some nights I go to bed and swear to myself that the next time she gets herself in a fix I'm going to force her to get herself out of it."

"I've had plenty of those same kinds of nights," he replied. "I know Justin drinks too much and he's irresponsible. I know he makes bad choices, and most of the time I clean them up for him. But just about the time I decide to wash my hands of him, I get a vision in my head of my old man beating the crap out of him when he was about six, and I remember I made myself a promise that I'd always take care of Justin."

She heard the tension in his voice and realized he'd gone to a dark place in his mind with his memories of his father. "It was a tough childhood," he continued. "Every morning I'd wake up and wonder if that was the day my dad was going to kill either me or one of my brothers."

"What a terrible way to live," she replied softly.

"It was, and the worst part was we never saw it coming. Dad was mercurial with his moods. I remember one night at dinner we were all sitting at the table. It had been a relatively pleasant day and Dad seemed to be in a pretty good mood. Then Justin reached for the bowl of mashed potatoes. Dad backhanded him so hard his chair tipped over backward and Justin crashed to the floor. He got up, got settled back in his chair, and Dad asked him if he wanted more of what he'd just gotten. Justin said no, but he'd still like to have some more mashed potatoes."

Jake shook his head and released a small laugh. "Justin never did know when to stop playing the fool."

Grace's heart hurt for the little boys they

had been. She couldn't imagine a childhood like what they had endured. "What happened?"

Jake shrugged. "Dad passed him the potatoes and the meal went on as if nothing had happened." He leaned back in his chair and drew a deep breath, then released it on a weary wind of resignation. "I know I cut him too much slack, run to his rescue way too often. There are times I just can't get the vision of him as a kid out of my head."

"But he's not a kid anymore," Grace said gently. "He's a man. It was different for me and Natalie," she said, trying to ease some of the darkness in his eyes. "I recognized fairly early that my mother wasn't capable of giving me the emotional support and love that I needed. I also realized fairly young that it was not a problem with me, but rather a problem with her."

"That's a pretty astute thing for a kid to figure out." He got up to pour himself more coffee.

"Mom was different with Natalie, more involved with her but not in the ways Natalie needed most. Mom would buy things for Natalie, spoil her with expensive items and toys, but she never gave Natalie what she needed most, which was her time and love."

"And so you have tried to make up for that with your sister." He returned to the table and offered her a rueful smile. "We're quite a pair, you know. Both of us trying to heal the damage our parents inflicted on our siblings." His smile faded as he looked at the girls in their high chairs. "He's never going to be what they need in their lives. I just don't think he's capable."

She nodded. "I know that now, and that's okay. I can't force him to be something he isn't." She raised a hand to her throat. "Now I just want to know if Shirley was the one who tried to kill me. It would be nice if I left in the morning with some kind of closure about what really happened here."

"I'm hoping Greg will have some news for us sometime today. Are you sure you'll be well enough to head home in the morning?"

Experimentally she moved her shoulder and winced slightly. "It's still sore, but much better than it's been. I think I'll be fine. If I need help when I get home I'll arrange for some." She stared at him for a long moment and once again her love for him buoyed up inside her, pressing tight against her chest.

"It's time for me to go home, Jake." She had to leave, because she so desperately didn't want to leave him.

He opened his mouth as if he wanted to say something, and then closed it again and nodded. By that time the girls were finished with their breakfast. "Da-da," Bonnie said to Jake and held out her arms.

"Don't worry, she doesn't mean it," Grace said as she carried her plate to the sink, rinsed it and placed it in the dishwasher. "Most babies say 'da-da' pretty regularly. It's an easy sound for them to make. We'll just get them settled in the living room for some playtime and you can take care of whatever chores you need to do."

"I'm not doing any chores today. I'm not leaving your side, Grace. I told you last night that I'd make sure nothing else happened to you while you were here and I meant it. My ranch hands can take care of anything that needs attention outside. Today it's just you and me and the girls."

He grabbed Bonnie from the high chair and then filled his other arm with Abby. There was nothing more appealing that a man dressed in babies, Grace thought as she carefully picked up Casey, using her good arm to do most of the work.

They got the girls settled in the living room. At that moment Grace's cell phone rang. She dug it out of her robe pocket, pleased to see on the caller ID that it was Natalie.

"Hey, sis," she said, trying to ignore how cute Jake looked seated on the floor with the girls. "I'm glad to finally hear from you."

"I was busy all day yesterday. I got a job," Natalie said.

"Natalie, that's wonderful! Where? Doing what?"

"It's just a waitressing job, but it's at a nice restaurant and the tips are decent and I kind of like it."

"But that's great," Grace exclaimed. "There's nothing wrong with waitressing, and at least it will give you a reason to get up in the mornings." *And hopefully a sense of responsibility,* Grace thought.

"So, what's up with you? When are you coming home? I miss you."

Grace smiled at her sister's words. "I miss you, too. And I'm planning on heading home first thing in the morning, so I should be there by noon at the latest."

"I'm working until five or so. I'll stop by your place as soon as I get off. Nothing has changed between you and Justin?"

"I've never met a man less likely to step up to be a father, so no, nothing has changed."

"Sorry about that. Kiss the girls for me and I'll see you tomorrow."

"I will," Grace agreed. She hung up and smiled at Jake. "She got a job."

"Congratulations," he replied. "That's got to be a relief."

"It is. She started yesterday, waitressing someplace. Let's just hope she can keep it for more than a week. Natalie has always been fairly good at getting jobs, it's been keeping them that's been the issue."

"Maybe this time will be different."

"Famous last words," she said and flashed him a rueful smile.

"Now, why don't you run upstairs and get dressed for the day while I watch the munch-kins," he suggested. "Because I've got to tell you the truth, seeing you in that silky robe through breakfast has made my mind wander to places it definitely shouldn't."

"Oh." Grace's cheeks filled with heat. "And maybe while I do that you should pull on a shirt so I don't have the same problem," she replied and then turned and hurried up the stairs.

Desire for Jake nipped at her heels as she raced into her bedroom, a healthy desire coupled with the quieter, wondrous feeling of love.

She had somebody who wanted to kill her and she was in love with the brother of the man who had fathered her children, a man who had made it clear in every way possible that she would never have a place in his life. Grace knew with a painful certainty that one way or another she wasn't going to leave here unscathed.

* * *

"The sheriff told me and Shirley to stay away," Justin exclaimed, his voice slightly slurred as if he'd already had too much to drink. "He said Grace was attacked last night and he thinks maybe me or Shirley had something to do with it. Jake, what in the hell is going on?"

Jake pressed the cell phone closer to his ear. "Where were you both last night?"

"I was home in bed, and I assume Shirley was home in her bed. I left her place around eleven, tired of all the drama. She kept going on and on about how much baggage the kids were going to be and when were we going to get married and have our own kids and stuff like that. Jake, I'll be the first to admit that Shirley wasn't exactly happy to learn about Grace and the kids, but she wouldn't try to kill Grace. You know me, Jake, and you've known Shirley most of her life. How could you believe such a thing of either one of us?"

Jake had already heard from Greg earlier in the day that Justin and Shirley's alibis for the night before were shaky at best.

He glanced in the kitchen where the girls were once again in their high chairs and Grace was finishing up the dinner preparations. "I don't know what to believe, Justin," he finally said. "The only thing I know for sure is that twice somebody has tried to harm Grace, and I intend to make sure she stays safe until she leaves here to go home. If I were you and Shirley I'd make sure until Grace leaves town you're in the company of other people so you have a solid alibi if anything else happens."

Jake knew his words were harsh, but he

wanted his brother to understand the reality of the situation. Greg was looking for an attempted murderer, and at the moment the only two suspects on his list were Justin and Shirley. Jake simply couldn't believe his brother had anything to do with this, but he wasn't so sure about Shirley.

"Where are you now, Justin?"

"Me and Shirley are at Tony's having a few brews."

"You really think that's a good idea? Maybe it's time you do a little less drinking, Justin. Maybe a stint in rehab wouldn't hurt."

"Whoa, buddy," Justin said with a forced laugh. "You're in a foul mood."

Jake released a tired sigh. "No, I'm not in a foul mood, Justin. I just want what's best for you and everyone else concerned. Sooner or later you're going to have to figure out how you're going to handle all this. But, for now, Greg is right. You and Shirley need to stay away from here."

"Problems?" Grace asked when he'd said goodbye to his brother and entered the kitchen.

"No, everything is fine," he assured her. The only real problem he'd had all day was his nearness to her. Watching her interact with the girls, enjoying the warmth of her smiles, the very fragrance of her, and remembering the fire of their kiss had set him on slow burn throughout the entire day. "Something in here smells good."

"Meat loaf, homemade mac and cheese, and peas," she replied as she stirred the peas simmering in a pot on the stove.

"Anything I can do to help?"

"Just sit and relax. I've got it all ready to put on the table."

He sat, but it was almost impossible to relax as he watched her bustling about. *She'll be gone tomorrow.* The words jumped into his head unbidden, as they had off and on throughout the afternoon.

It's what you want, he reminded himself. All he'd ever wanted since the moment she'd arrived was to be out of her drama and left alone. Tomorrow morning he would get his wish, and he couldn't understand why he didn't feel completely happy at the prospect.

Maybe it was just because he didn't like mysteries, and the gunshots and the attack in the bedroom were certainly mysteries that hadn't been solved. And it didn't look as if they were going to be solved before she left town.

"You're very quiet," she said once she had everything on the table and had joined him there.

"I was just thinking that it's going to be pretty quiet around here once you and the girls leave." As if to punctuate his sentence, Bonnie squealed in delight as Grace set her plate of mac and cheese, and peas in front of her. The other two reacted in much the same way then grew silent as they began to eat.

"I'll bet you can't wait to get your house back to the peace and quiet it was before we arrived," Grace said.

"Yeah, right," he replied, not meeting her gaze as he began to fill his plate. Peace and quiet, that's what he wanted. No babies crawling on him, drooling kisses or giggling with glee. No hair or ear pulling, no batting eyelashes, nothing that would bring a smile to his lips or any warmth of connection to his heart.

No Grace scent muddying his mind, twisting him inside out with feelings he'd never had before. It would just be plain stupid to allow anything to develop with Grace and the girls. It would be counterproductive to everything he'd decided he wanted in his life.

"It's too bad Greg didn't have a definitive answer for you about the attacks before you left," he said when the silence between them had stretched for too long.

She paused with a forkful of macaroni and cheese halfway to her mouth. "He could call with an answer before I go in the morning. I don't believe your brother was behind the attacks, Jake. However, my verdict is still out on Shirley. There was no question that she thought I was somehow a threat to her relationship with Justin." Her green eyes darkened. "I guess that kind of jealousy and desperation can make an unstable woman capable of almost anything. Besides, it's the only thing that makes any kind of sense. I'm fairly certain that once I leave here tomorrow I won't hear from Justin again and Shirley will have no reason to feel threatened anymore."

Jake wished he could protest her words, tell her that he was sure his brother would not only get in contact with her but would be a supportive presence in his daughters' lives. But at this point he knew they would just be empty words.

The only thing they knew for sure about the attack was that a red bandana had been used as the gag in Grace's mouth, and they were sold at every store in the area.

And tomorrow she would be gone.

Jake felt as if there was an invisible presence in the room that made itself known in a sizzling burn in the pit of his gut.

Desire. It had chased him through the house all day, ached deep inside him as they finished the meal. It whispered want to him as they cleaned up the kitchen, and it grew noisier in his head two hours later when they put the girls down to sleep for the night.

There was a part of him that believed that if he had her, if he made love with her just one time, then she'd be out of his system for good and it would be easier for him to tell her goodbye the next morning.

But there was another part of him that feared it would never be enough, that if he made love to her once then he would want to repeat it again and again. And she represented everything he didn't want in his life.

With the girls in their cribs for the night, they went back down to the living room where she sat on the sofa and he sat in the chair opposite her. He wanted to maintain as much physical distance from her as possible and yet be in the same room.

"I'm sorry things worked out the way they did for you here," he said. "You know you could take Justin to court, force him to at least pay child support."

"I would if it meant my babies having something or nothing," she replied. "I absolutely believe every child has a right to have the financial support of both parents. But in this case, the girls are well taken care of. And, to be honest, I'm ready to walk away from Justin and not look back."

A flash of pain crossed her features. "He's obviously not ready to be a father, and making him pay child support isn't going to change that. Someday he'll have to answer to the girls, but he doesn't have to answer to me."

"You're a strong woman."

She smiled and nodded. "Yes, I am. And you're a strong man, and I hope the day comes when you can stop carrying the sins of your father on your back."

He sat up straighter and looked at her in surprise. "I'm not doing that," he protested.

"Of course you are," she countered. "I think we've both been doing more than our share of that," she replied. "Trying to make up to Natalie and Justin for things they didn't get in their childhoods, things we didn't get in our childhoods. Personally, I plan on making some changes when I get home where Natalie is concerned. She's going to have to learn to stand on her own. It's past time I cut the cord. I have three baby girls to focus my energy on."

"And what happens in the fall when you go back to work?"

"They go to a terrific day care." She gazed off into space thoughtfully. "I have to admit there's a part of me that would love to be a stay-at-home mom until they got to be school-age. I have my contract for working next fall sitting at home on my desk. I haven't signed it yet. I love teaching, but I'm also aware that I can't get back the girls' toddler years. I'm lucky in that if I don't live lavishly and am smart, I can afford to make a decision rather than the decision being forced on me."

"Whatever choice you make, I'm sure it will

be a good one. You strike me as a woman who only makes good choices."

She smiled with a touch of humor. "Don't forget there were two of us in that bed when the triplets were conceived. I acted as stupid and reckless as Justin did that night. I'm ashamed to admit I hardly have any memories at all after a certain point in the evening, but there's no question that I decided to throw caution to the wind and let the booze and Justin sweep me away."

"Tell me more about this MysteryMom who brought you here." He knew she was probably eager to go to bed so she could get an early start in the morning, but he wasn't ready to tell her good-night. There was a part of him that wasn't ready to tell her goodbye.

"I don't know a lot about her personal life. I connected with her in a chat room for pregnant and single women. I just lurked for about a week and I noticed that she gave good advice, seemed knowledgeable about pregnancy and single parenting. She even gave one of the women in the chat room enough information to help her find the father of her baby who had disappeared when he'd found out she was pregnant. I finally started posting and told a little bit about my situation. Then MysteryMom and I started emailing each other outside of the chat room."

"And you became friends," he replied.

She nodded. "Cyberfriends. Good friends. Especially when I found out I was having triplets. I was more than a little freaked out, and she saw me through some of my rough moments."

He wished he would have been there for her, when she needed somebody to rub her tired back, when she just wanted somebody to talk to, to fix her a cup of tea or whatever. "I'm sorry you had to go through it all alone except for the support of a cyberfriend."

"I have a feeling even if I'd found Justin the day I discovered I was pregnant I would have still gone through it all alone," she returned.

"What about other friends?" he asked.

"I have acquaintances, but true friendships have been a little difficult to maintain. First there was my involvement in Natalie's life, then the triplets' arrival pretty much chased away any of my other single women friends."

"That stinks," he replied.

She smiled. "Not really. It was mostly my fault. I was just too busy to be a friend." She raised a hand and yawned. "And now I should probably call it a night. I'd like to get an early start in the morning."

She got up from the sofa and a wild panic shot through Jake. These were the last moments they would have together alone. He knew she was right, that once she returned to Wichita the odds of them maintaining any kind of relationship were minimal. He'd send birthday presents to the girls, call to check in on them every once in a while, but for all intents and purposes his connection with Grace would be severed.

And that's what you want, he reminded himself as he got out of his chair. He'd said goodbye to dozens of women in his lifetime, and she should be no different than any of them.

And yet she was different, a little voice whispered in the very depths of his soul. The other women who had drifted in and out of his life hadn't made his heartache for something undefined, something he felt he needed and yet found that very need frightening.

"Go ahead and sleep in my bed again tonight," he said as they walked toward the stairs. "I'll bunk in Jeffrey and Kerri's room again." He didn't want her anywhere near the room with the sliding glass door, and he would sleep with one eye open throughout the night.

He'd taken necessary precautions to make sure that nobody got close to the house again. Jimbo was camping out on the front porch for the night, and Rick Carson, another ranch hand, was bunking down on the back porch. *Bunking down* wasn't really the right term. Both men had promised to keep their eyes and ears open throughout the dark hours of the night, and Jake trusted those men as much as he trusted anyone in his life.

Jake would stick to his promise; he'd keep her safe and sound until she left here to go home. As they climbed the stairs, he tried not to inhale the familiar scent of her that called to every raging male hormone in his body. He tried not to imagine that he could feel the heat of her calling to him, wanting to share with him.

As always she stopped in the girls' room and checked each little child. He thought of Bonnie's flirting with him, of how Casey tucked her head down when feeling particularly shy, of Abby laughing with delight as he played peekaboo with her. Grace wasn't the only female here who had found her way into his heart. Each and every one of the triplets had also crawled into tiny places that would make them hard to forget when they were gone.

How had this happened? How had he allowed them all to get so close? They weren't his…they were never meant to be his.

"Then I guess this is good night," he said when they finally reached the door to his room.

"It doesn't have to be good night," she replied. The green of her eyes shone overly bright in the hallway light.

"What do you mean?" His pulse stepped up its rhythm.

"You could sleep in here with me."

Her words, so unexpected and so enticing, caused his heart to momentarily skip a beat. His head filled with a vision of her between his sheets, her lips swollen from his kisses and her naked body pressed against his.

"Grace…" He wasn't sure what he intended to say, but his voice came out as a hoarse whisper. He needed strength, but he wanted to be weak.

"Tonight we make love and we sleep in each other's arms, but you don't have to worry about anything changing, Jake." Her eyes shone with both desire and a promise. "I still leave here in the morning. You still get your life of being alone."

Wrong. It was all wrong, his conscience suggested. *You're strong enough to resist this temptation. You need to be strong enough to resist.* But he wasn't. He was weak where Grace was concerned, and at the moment he couldn't think of anything he'd rather do than make love to her.

Big mistake, he thought as he followed her into the familiar bedroom that suddenly felt like a strange and wondrous place.

Chapter 10

As Jake turned on the lamp next to the bed, Grace took off her sling and placed it on the nearby chair. Her hands trembled slightly as she thought about what she was about to do.

There was absolutely no doubt in her mind that they were going to make love. She wanted this, she wanted him, and even ultimately knowing that it was going to be just another one-night stand with a Johnson man couldn't change her mind.

She was doing this for herself, making a

memory that would bring a smile to her lips, a warmth to her heart when she needed it in the weeks and months ahead.

Somebody had tried to kill her, and just for a little while, just for tonight, she wanted to pretend that somebody loved her.

Jake stood inches from her, frozen except for the burning hunger in his eyes, a hunger that filled her up with a heat she'd never known before.

"You don't have to worry. I'm on birth control," she said, wanting to get that issue settled right up front. There would be no set of triplets or even a single baby made tonight.

He took a step toward her, her breasts making contact with his broad chest. "This isn't right," he said, his voice low and filled with deep longing.

"But it isn't wrong, either," she countered.

"We're both single. Our hearts belong to nobody. I want you, Jake. I want this before I leave here tomorrow."

His mouth crashed to hers at the same time he wound his arms around her and pulled her against him, and just that easily she was lost in him.

There was no thought of going home, or of taking care of babies. There was no worry about her sister or who might have tried to hurt her. There was only Jake. Sweet, strong Jake.

His scent smelled like home, like sweet comfort, and his kiss tasted of hot, wild desire. Everything seemed to be happening in a dream, a wonderful dream that she wanted to last forever.

She didn't remember taking off her clothes, but found herself naked in his bed. She didn't remember seeing him undress, but he was also naked with her beneath the sheet, his body all hot muscle beside her.

As he drew her into his arms for another searing kiss, her hands caressed the width of his back, loving the feel of muscle and hot flesh beneath her fingertips.

He kissed just as she'd imagined he would, with intensity, with command and yet with a gentleness that melted her senses even more.

A small moan escaped her as his lips left hers and began to blaze an exploratory trail down the side of her throat, along the line of her collarbone. When his tongue lightly flicked across one of her taut nipples, a flash fire of sensation shot through her.

His hands cupped her breasts as his tongue loved first one nipple then the other. Tangling her fingers in his thick hair, she was lost to everything except the man and his caresses.

One of his hands left her breast and began to stroke slowly, languidly down her stomach. Every muscle in her body tensed with the anticipation of his intimate touch.

Teasingly, he slid his fingers down the outside of her thigh, then moved to the inside of her thigh and stopped just short of where she wanted him most, where she needed him most.

She mewled in frustration and was rewarded by his husky chuckle. "This is a one-shot deal, Grace. I don't want to be in a hurry. I want us to take our time. I want this to last all night long."

His words caused a shiver of delight to race up her spine. Yes, she wanted to be in his arms, with his hands and lips touching her all night long.

When he gazed at her with those dark, intense eyes, when he stroked her skin with his slightly work roughened hands, she felt like the most beautiful woman on the face of the earth. No man had ever looked at her the way he did. No man made her feel like she did at this time.

There was a moment as his lips drank of hers that thoughts of leaving intruded, that her heart folded into itself in anticipation of the pain it would feel the next morning when she bid him a final goodbye and drove away from here.

Still, she shoved the thought away, not wanting to think, just wanting to feel, to be in this moment with this man.

He was fully aroused, his hardness pressed

against her thigh, and she reached down and wrapped her fingers around his velvet soft skin, eliciting a low, deep moan from him.

She felt him throbbing in her grasp and loved that she was doing that to him, that she had him so aroused and ready to take her.

And she wanted him to take her. A sweet urgency of need sizzled through her as they continued to touch and taste each other.

She cried out in pleasure as his fingers finally found the center of her, moving against the sensitive skin and calling forth a tidal wave of pleasure. As the wave rushed over her his name escaped her lips as her body shuddered with the force.

His eyes shone with satisfaction as the shudders finally stopped and she released a sigh of sated pleasure. But he wasn't finished yet.

He rolled on top of her and she opened her

thighs to welcome him, her need rising once again as his mouth found hers in a kiss that seared her soul.

Still kissing, he eased into her and released a sigh of utter bliss. "I think I've wanted this since the moment I first saw you," he whispered.

She closed her eyes, not wanting to see the depth of emotion his contained, knowing that it was the emotion of the moment, one that would be gone when their lovemaking was over.

He moved inside her and her breath caught in her chest at the sensual assault. Then there was no more thought as their hips moved together, friction firing up a wildness that consumed her.

Her second orgasm washed over her as she clung to his shoulders. While she was still trembling with the force of it she felt him reach his own.

As sweet as her joy was, the sudden depth of her despair at the knowledge that it was over whispered through her made tears burn at her eyes.

"Hey, you okay?"

She opened her eyes to see him gazing down at her, a look of concern on his face. She swallowed against the threat of tears and offered him a smile. "After that how could I not be okay?"

For several long seconds they held each other's gazes. She wondered if he could see the love shining in her eyes. Unfortunately, she couldn't read his; they remained dark and enigmatic.

He kissed her then, a deep kiss that tasted of love and yet also held more than a whisper of goodbye. When the kiss ended she rolled out from under him and went into the bathroom.

Minutes later she stood in front of the bathroom mirror and stared at her reflection. If it wasn't insane, she would pack up the girls at that moment and leave with the scent of him still clinging to her skin, with the taste of him still sweet in her mouth. She would leave before she spent the rest of the night in his arms, letting him dig deeper into her heart.

But she wasn't going to drag her girls out in the middle of the night. And she wasn't going to deprive herself of the rest of this night, even though she knew each moment she spent with Jake would only make the pain of leaving in the morning worse.

It was crazy, wasn't it? To even want a future with him—to see him as the soul mate she'd always dreamed of. It was stupid and weird to believe that there could ever be a future with the brother of the father of her children.

When she left the bathroom and got back into bed, Jake immediately pulled her into his arms. She smelled the soapy scent of him and realized he'd washed up as well.

He turned out the bedside lamp and she fit neatly into the spoon of his body. Once again she found herself giving in to him, settling into his arms as if it was where she belonged.

"Did I hurt your shoulder?" he asked, the words a soft whisper just behind her ear.

"No, it's fine."

"Are you sure you don't need to hang around here another day or two to let it heal a little more before you head back?" he asked.

What she wanted was to hang around here

another ten, twenty, fifty years. She wanted to be with Jake for the rest of her life. She wanted him to be the father of the triplets. But that was fantasy thinking, foolish wistfulness.

"I should be able to handle going home tomorrow with no problem," she replied.

"I have to confess there's a part of me that's going to miss you and the girls." His arms tightened around her.

She held her breath, waiting for, desperately wanting something more from him. *Just ask me to stay,* she inwardly begged. *Just tell me you want me and the girls in your life forever.*

A long silence grew, and then she realized he'd fallen asleep.

Squeezing her eyes closed, she realized with a heart-sickening finality what she'd known the first time she'd met Justin—that there was nothing for her here.

Jake awoke early, before dawn had even begun to streak tentative light across the sky. Grace was no longer in his arms, but rather sleeping soundly, curled up in a fetal position on the opposite side of the bed. He wished there was enough light so he could watch her sleeping. To fill his heart with the sight of her, her hair sleep-tousled and all the worry gone from her face.

He crept out of the bed without waking her, grabbed his clothes for the day and then walked quietly down the hallway to the other bathroom in order to shower and dress without bothering her.

She was leaving today. She was taking her children and leaving his house. Things would go back to the way they had been before she'd arrived.

He should be happy, but as he stepped beneath the hot spray of the shower, happiness wasn't the emotion that resonated through him.

As he washed away the scent of her, all he could think of was what a mess this had all become. He hoped that if Shirley was responsible for the attacks on Grace then Greg would get evidence of it and Shirley would face the consequences.

In the very depths of his soul he thought she was the likely culprit. He just didn't want to believe that Justin had played a role in the attacks in any way.

But if nothing else had come out of this time with Grace, Jake now realized he needed to let go of his brother. It was time for Justin to stand or fall on his own.

Grace had been right when she'd told him he'd been carrying the sins of his father for too long. Nothing he could do would fix the childhood the three men had endured, a childhood they had all endured together. It was time to let go of the responsibility and let Justin be a man.

After he'd showered and dressed and left the bathroom, he thought he heard a sound from the girls' room. One peek into the room and he saw Bonnie peering over the top of her crib, her wide smile sliding straight into his heart as she raised her arms to him.

Seeing that the other two were still sleeping, he hurried to her crib and picked her up. He didn't speak to her until he'd left the room.

"You're a little early bird this morning," he said as he carried her down the stairs.

She bounced on his hip and wrapped her arms around his neck, as if delighted to have him all to herself. He was going to miss them. He'd never thought it possible, but he was going to miss seeing the triplets' smiling faces first thing in the morning, hearing their babble and giggles filling the house.

As he placed Bonnie in one of the high chairs in the kitchen, he didn't even want to think about how much he was going to miss Grace.

Always before the thought of silence in the house had filled him with a sense of pleasure. But when he thought about how quiet the house would be with the triplets and Grace gone, his heart pressed painful and tight in his chest.

They weren't his issue. They'd never been his issue, he reminded himself. Justin and circumstances out of his control had put him in the middle of this, and he should be grateful that within hours he'd be out of the middle of it all.

He gave Bonnie a handful of the round oat cereal he'd seen Grace give her before, then set about making a pot of coffee. As he waited for the brew to drip through, he stood at the window and watched dawn break across the sky, aware that the minutes of Grace and the girls being here in the house were ticking away.

He knew she cared about him. It was obvious in the way she looked at him, in the very fact that she'd made love with him the night before. She cared about him a lot, might even fancy herself in love with him.

But he couldn't help but wonder if most of her attraction to him was because he looked like Justin, because she could fantasize just by looking at him that he was her daughters' father.

When he'd held her in his arms last night and she'd closed her eyes, had she imagined that he was his brother? Had she pretended that it was Justin kissing her, Justin loving her? After all, Jake was the version of Justin she'd probably like to have.

He shook his head to dislodge the thought. At this point what did it matter? Justin wasn't going to suddenly become the man she needed in her life. Jake wasn't going to abandon his own dreams. She was leaving. Within weeks Jeffrey and Kerri would be moved out, and he'd decided moments before that from now on Justin would truly be on his own.

The future he'd always dreamed for himself was a mere stone's throw away. All he had to do was get through the goodbyes of this morning and the rest of his life would fall into place.

He heard the water start running someplace upstairs and knew that Grace was up. *Another early riser probably eager to get back to her real life,* he thought as a hard knot formed in the pit of his stomach.

She'd been fine before she'd come here, and there was no reason for him to believe that she wouldn't be fine when she left. She was a strong woman, had apparently had to be strong all her life. He didn't need to worry about her.

Minutes later she came into the kitchen. "Looks as if I'm not the only early riser," she said as she dropped a kiss on Bonnie's forehead and then moved to the coffeemaker on the countertop.

"Did you sleep well?" he asked, trying not to notice how pretty she looked in a pair of jeans and a jewel-green blouse that electrified the green of her eyes.

"Very well," she replied. As she turned to pour herself a cup of coffee, he fought the impulse to step up behind her and press his lips against the nape of her neck.

He wondered if it was just an effort to somehow continue the intimacy they'd shared the night before.

When she turned to face him he was glad he hadn't, for there was a distance in her eyes that let him know she was already gone. Mentally and emotionally she was already back on the road headed home.

"You want some breakfast?" he asked.

She shook her head and carried her cup to the table. "No, when Abby and Casey wake up I'll feed them before we take off, but I'm really not hungry."

He remained standing at the window. "Going to be a beautiful day for your drive home."

"I'm just looking forward to getting home and back into my own routine."

"How's the shoulder?"

She moved it experimentally. "Still a little stiff and sore, but manageable. We'll be fine, Jake."

"I know," he replied. "I'm just sorry it has to be this way. I'm sorry you didn't get what you came here for where Justin is concerned."

She offered him a small smile. "I told you before, you don't owe me any apologies on his behalf. Besides, nothing ventured, nothing gained, right?" She took a sip of her coffee and then placed the mug on the table. "The good thing is I know where to come if any health issues should arise with the girls and I need answers. They will know where they come from. I won't have to have the embarrassment of telling them I don't know who or where their father is. Eventually Justin will probably have to deal with them one way or another, but there's nothing more I can do here." She released a deep sigh. "I'm ready to go home."

At that moment one of the other girls upstairs cried out and officially the day began. It was just after nine when the triplets had been fed, the car had been loaded and there was nothing left to do except tell her goodbye.

He stood at her driver's side door and watched as she slid behind the wheel. There was a part of him that wanted to stop her, to tell her that somehow, someway, she'd gotten under his skin, delved into his heart in a way he hadn't expected.

He wanted to pull her out from behind the steering wheel and grab her, feel the warmth of her against him once again and tell her that he didn't want her to leave. But his body refused to follow through on the thought.

"Bye-bye," Bonnie said, and the other two little girls echoed the sentiment.

"And I think that's my cue," Grace said as she started the engine. "I left my address and phone numbers on a piece of paper on the kitchen table for Justin. If he ever decides he wants to discuss the girls or come and see them, then all he needs to do is call me and we'll set something up."

"Grace?" He wasn't sure what he wanted to say, but he was fairly sure it wasn't goodbye.

"Yes?" For a moment in the depths of her eyes he saw something shiny and bright, something that made him feel if she drove out of his driveway it would be the worst thing that ever happened to him. Yet he wasn't willing to change anything.

"Drive safely," he finally said.

The light in her eyes dimmed slightly, and she put the car into gear. "I will." She drew a deep breath. "Jake, you're a man who is meant to be a husband and a father. This big house was meant to be filled with family. You've spent the first half of your life fixing everybody else's. Don't spend the last half of your life running away from your own."

She didn't wait for him to reply but stepped on the gas and shot down the driveway as if chased by the devil himself. He watched until the car disappeared from his vision and only then turned and headed back inside.

The utter silence of the house should have embraced him with welcoming arms. He walked through the living room and heard only the sound of his own beating heart.

It's what he'd always wanted. It's what he'd dreamed of. Tomorrow Kerri and Jeffrey would be home, and he doubted that he'd hear from Justin anytime soon. He'd have the house and the silence to himself for the remainder of the day.

The sight of the three high chairs in the kitchen speared a surprising feeling of loss through his heart. For the last couple of days they'd felt like his children.

And Grace had felt like his woman.

But I don't want a woman, he told himself

as he sank down at the table. And he didn't want children. He didn't want the mess, the fuss and the noise. He didn't want the dramas or the responsibilities that came with relationships and parenthood. He'd done enough where that was concerned.

Peace and quiet. What more could a man ask for? He picked up the sheet of paper where Grace had written her address and phone numbers.

By all rights she should have run as fast and as far as she could after her first meeting with Justin, but she hadn't. She'd stuck around to give him a second chance. She'd desperately wanted a father for her daughters. She told him she knew what it was like to grow up without one, and that wasn't what she wanted for her babies.

Of all the men in the world she could have

fallen into bed with at a wedding, why did it have to be Justin, who would probably never find it within himself to be what Grace and the girls needed?

He leaned back in the chair and closed his eyes, playing and replaying each and every moment he'd spent with her and the triplets.

He made himself a mental note to call Greg later in the day to see if he had any news about the attacks. Even though Grace was gone, Jake still wanted the guilty party found. And if it had been Shirley, then Justin would be crazy to stick with a woman capable of that kind of thing.

Grace had told him that it had been a near-death experience that had made her decide to come here to the ranch in the first place, and then she'd gone from the frying pan into the fire by being attacked here.

He opened his eyes and sat up straighter with a frown. She'd told him she'd been forced off the road a couple of days before coming here. It had only been by the grace of God that her car hadn't flipped over and killed her. It had been a close call.

His brain suddenly fired with all kinds of suppositions. Was it possible that the shooting had been the second attempt on Grace's life? That the first attempt had been that night in Wichita before she'd ever left to come here?

If that was the case, then it changed every-thing. That had happened before Justin even knew about the triplets, before Shirley had known anything about Grace and Justin's night together.

His heart began beating an unnatural rhythm of stress. If that was the case, then it meant somebody had tried to kill her in

Wichita and then had followed her here to try again.

And if that was true, then that meant she wasn't driving back to safety but rather was driving back into danger.

Chapter 11

Alone.

Grace had been alone most of her life. When she'd been young she'd learned to give herself the comfort and love she didn't get from her mother. She certainly got little true companionship or caring from her sister.

The triplets filled her heart and soul like nobody and nothing ever had before, but they weren't meant to fill the loneliness that had been a part of Grace's life for as long as she could remember.

Jake had filled that space, that loneliness, and more than that there had been several times when he'd given her a touch of crazy hope that there might be something there with him for her and her girls.

Until the moment she'd put her car into gear, that little touch of hope had shimmered in her heart. He'd spoken her name with such wanting, and her heart had nearly stopped in anticipation of him pulling her out of the car and telling her he loved her and the girls. But he'd let her drive away, and by the time she'd reached the end of the ranch's driveway, tears raced down her cheeks.

It had been crazy for her to even think for one minute that he'd want to take on her and the triplets, that somehow he'd fallen in love with her and that love was deep enough for him to throw his own wants, his own needs, away.

Alone. She was going to be alone for a long time to come. It would take a very special man to want to take on not just her, but her three daughters as well. She was a woman who came with baggage, three little suitcases who babbled and drooled, who would grow up to walk and get into things and create chaos.

For just a stupid, crazy moment she'd thought that special man was Jake. She raised a hand from the steering wheel to swipe at an errant tear.

She felt half-sick to her stomach with the pain that pierced through her center. She never knew heartache could be such a physical pain.

It was her own fault that she was leaving here with a broken heart. She'd allowed him to get too close, had opened her heart to him as she'd never opened her heart to a man before.

She had the two-and-a-half-hour drive to pull herself together, to shove thoughts of Jake out of her mind and focus on her real life.

At least Natalie had a job. Maybe it was time Grace took some of the advice she had given Jake. It was time for her to stop rescuing Natalie, stop trying to make up for the lack of a father and the less-than-perfect relationship with her mother.

Natalie had her monthly income from her inheritance, and with even a part-time job she should do fine as long as she learned to stop partying and live within her means.

Grace could only hope the Jimmy she was dating was a good and decent young man, but it was time Grace took her own advice and stopped rescuing her sister.

She frowned, wondering what damage Natalie had managed to do to the credit card she'd let her use. Supposedly Natalie had just needed gas money and groceries, but there was no telling what Grace might find charged on the card when she finally got the bill.

It didn't take long for the lull of the wheels on the pavement to put the girls to sleep, leaving Grace alone with her thoughts. And they were all of Jake.

He had been everything she'd ever dreamed of in a man for herself, everything she'd ever dreamed of as a father for her children. It was as if Bonnie had identified Jake as somebody important in their lives the first time she'd batted her eyelashes at him. Watching him with them had filled Grace's soul with a sense of rightness.

He'd loved the girls like Grace had hoped their father would. When he'd played with them, wiped their mouths, laughed at their antics, there had been a feeling of family, a warmth that had filled Grace's soul.

Grace blinked away a new flurry of tears. What she didn't understand was how she could feel such loss when she'd never really had him to begin with. They had played house for a couple of days due to circumstances beyond their control.

Everything he had done for her while she'd been at the ranch had probably been part of him doing what he always did—taking care of Justin's messes.

She jumped as her cell phone rang. With one hand she dug it out of her purse and looked at the caller ID. Jake. The very last person in the world she wanted to talk to at the moment.

Why would he be calling? To tell her she left something behind? She was fairly sure she'd gotten out of there with all her belongings. Her heart was a different story.

She didn't even want to hear his voice right now. She knew the sound would merely pull forth the tears she'd been desperately trying to hold back. She turned the phone off and dropped it back into her purse. She'd return his call later, when she was back home in her own environment and not feeling quite so vulnerable to him.

The girls' nap didn't last long. Within half an hour they were awake and chattering like magpies, filling the silence that had been in the car but incapable of soothing the hollow emptiness that resided in Grace's heart—the space where Jake had been.

By the time she pulled into her driveway she was grateful the drive was over. The girls had started to get cranky, needing lunch and a longer nap, and Grace's shoulder ached from the driving.

It took another hour to get everything unloaded from the car, feed the girls and get them down for their naps, and then she took one of the pain pills the doctor in Cameron Creek had given her and stretched out on her sofa.

There were a million things she should be doing, like throwing in a load of laundry, figuring out what she was going to have for supper or contacting MysteryMom to let her know that Justin had been found but was ultimately lost.

What she wouldn't confess to MysteryMom was that she'd been fool enough to fall in love with one of Justin's brothers. That she'd been fool enough to get pregnant by a man incapable of being a father and had fallen in love with a man incapable of loving her back.

Jake, her heart cried out as she closed her eyes and sought the oblivion of sleep. If nothing else she hoped that someday he would get over his own baggage and find love with somebody, build a family that would make him see that chaos and noise when filled with love was so much better than silence and being all alone.

She finally fell asleep with her heart aching, wondering how long it would take before she could forget all about Jake Johnson. She dreamed of him, of being held in his arms as they made love. The dream transitioned to him holding her babies and all of them laughing. Then she went from dreamland to sudden awakeness, her heart beating a frantic rhythm that had nothing to do with the visions that had filled her sleep.

Sitting up, she looked around and listened. No crying babies, nothing to indicate what had pulled her from sleep or had made her heart race so fast. A glance at her wristwatch let her know she'd only been asleep for about fifteen minutes.

It must have been a dream, she thought as she placed a hand over her pounding heart and drew a deep breath. She must have been having a dream that created the sense of panic that had awakened her.

At that moment Natalie appeared in the doorway between the kitchen and the living room.

Grace released a startled gasp and real-ized it must have been the sound of the back door opening and closing that had awakened her. "Jeez, Natalie, you scared me to half to death," she exclaimed. "I thought you told me you had to work today."

"I really don't like working," Natalie re-plied. "Life is too short to work, especially when I shouldn't have to." There was a tough edge to Natalie's voice and a wildness in her eyes.

"What are you doing sneaking in the back door?" Grace asked, her heart sinking as she realized it was possible her sister was on something. Grace's heart suddenly resumed its rapid beat. "Natalie, have you been doing drugs?"

"Maybe so, maybe not." Natalie grinned as a tall, lanky, dark-haired young man appeared just behind her. "You've been wanting to meet Jimmy, so here he is."

He stepped up next to Natalie. "Hey, Grace."

He didn't look like the decent kind of young man Grace had hoped for. He had a rough edge, made more rough by the tattoo that nearly covered one side of his neck and his general unkempt appearance. His jeans hung low and his hair was long and greasy.

"It's nice to finally meet you," Grace forced herself to say.

"You've been quite a problem," he said. His dark eyes looked as wild as Natalie's.

Grace frowned at him, wondering if the pain pill she'd taken earlier had somehow scrambled her brains or if she'd misunderstood him. "Excuse me?"

"He said you've become quite a problem,"

Natalie repeated with a touch of impatience. "Actually, you became a problem the minute you had those babies and Mother changed her will."

Grace watched in horror as Jimmy pulled a gun from the back of his waistband and pointed it at her. "Your sister and I want to be together. We love each other, but she's been very unhappy with her inheritance and I can't stand to see her so miserable."

Grace felt as if she was still asleep, in the middle of a terrible nightmare as her gaze went from Jimmy to her sister. "I don't understand. Natalie, you and I both got the same amount of an inheritance when Mom died." Grace struggled to make sense of what was happening.

"They got it all," Natalie said, her features showing the first signs of anger. Her green eyes narrowed and her chin thrust forward. "Those babies got everything, and that means *you've* got it all."

"That's not true," Grace exclaimed, a panic welling up to press tight against her chest. "It's for them, not for me. It's for their college."

"But you can get to it whenever you want," Natalie screamed. "You can just write a check and buy whatever you want with it. It's not fair. It was never fair."

Horrible thoughts suddenly tumbled around in Grace's head. She'd always known deep in her heart that Natalie was selfish and more than a bit narcissistic, but now she recognized the depth of Natalie's rage, a rage that had apparently been building since the reading of their mother's will.

Natalie drew a deep breath as if to calm

herself, but her eyes remained wild and filled with anger. "She promised me. Mother promised me when I was growing up that I'd have everything I wanted, that when she was gone I'd never want for anything. She promised and I believed her and you screwed it up by having those damned kids."

Grace searched her sister's features, looking for something soft, something vulnerable, something of the sister she thought she knew, but there was nothing there. The full realization of what lengths Natalie had gone to sank in. "*You* followed me to Cameron Creek? *You* tried to shoot me?" her voice was a mere whisper.

"If those stupid cowboys hadn't shown up when they did we wouldn't be having this conversation now," Natalie said.

"So far you've been like a cat with nine

lives." Jimmy stepped closer to her, the gun pointed at her head. "I tried to run you off the road, I tried to shoot you, and then I tried to strangle you. Each time you've managed to get away. Unfortunately, the cat has now run out of lives."

"Jimmy and I can take care of the girls," Natalie said as if she were talking about taking care of a couple of goldfish. "As their guardian I'll make sure they have what they need, but I can also live the life I want to live, the one I deserve to live."

"Natalie and I are going to live a great life. Unfortunately, you're in the way of that." Jimmy smiled, but there was no humor in the gesture. "Face it, sis. You have to go."

Grace looked at her sister, hoping this was all some kind of a terrible joke, but Natalie's eyes held a hard glaze she didn't recognize.

"I won't have to hear you bitch at me anymore. I won't have to listen to your stupid advice." Natalie's hands balled into fists at her side. "All the times I wanted Mother and she wasn't there for me, I always remembered that she told me it would be worth it in the end, that if anything happened to her I'd have a life most people dreamed about. I'm not going to let those brats take that away from me."

"While you were gone somebody cased your house," Jimmy said. "They broke in and didn't realize you were back home. As they started to rob the place, you confronted them and sadly you didn't survive the attack."

Horror rose up inside Grace's throat. "Natalie, you can't be serious about this. I'm your sister, for God's sake."

"I don't care about you," Natalie replied. "I just want the money."

"Even if you kill me, the girls have a father who would get custody," Grace said, trying to reason her way out of danger.

"He doesn't want custody," she scoffed. "You told me he isn't fit material to be a guardian. You told me the last thing he wants is to be a father. Trust me, from what you said about him he won't fight me. He'll be glad that somebody else is ready to step in to take care of them. I'm their aunt, your only living relative. I'll get custody and I'll get their money. The only thing that stands in my way is you."

As Grace looked into the very soullessness of her sister's eyes, she realized she'd vastly underestimated Natalie's mental problems and as a consequence she was in terrible danger.

* * *

Jake tried to call Grace several times, but each of his calls went directly to her voice mail. Since he couldn't imagine her risking driving while talking on the cell phone, he could only assume that she had the phone off.

Still, with each passing minute that took her closer to her home, an urgency banged in his heart. It was crazy for him to think she might be in imminent danger, and yet was it really so far-fetched?

Somebody had tried to kill her, and he'd begun to think it wasn't somebody from here but rather somebody close to her back in Wichita.

Even though he knew it was probably il-logical, he felt as if he needed to get to her as soon as possible, and without being able to call her, he did the next best thing. He grabbed the sheet of paper with her address on it, got into his truck and took off after her.

He was a good thirty or forty minutes behind her. It was possible if he pushed the speed limit he could catch her on the road. If not, he'd use the address she'd left and get to her house.

And tell her what? That a car accident might not have been an accident at all? That he thought somebody was chasing her all over the country in an effort to kill her? That somehow this made more sense than Shirley being responsible for the two attacks on her?

His foot eased off the gas pedal as doubts filled his head. Was he chasing after her with these crazy ideas because deep in his heart he didn't want to let her go?

Was his heart telling him something his brain refused to acknowledge? This time was it him creating drama instead of his brother? Chasing after a woman with some conspiracy plot just because he wanted to see her one more time?

No, this wasn't about some imagined drama. He pressed his foot back on the gas, once again filled with a sense of urgency. This had nothing to do with what he wanted or didn't want with Grace and the children. This had to do with their safety, and despite all rational thought, he felt that she was heading right into trouble.

As he passed each roadside café and gas station along the way, he slowed to look for her car but didn't see it parked anywhere. He could only press the speed limit so much. The last thing he wanted was to get reckless and be in an accident of his own or cause a problem for other drivers.

He consciously didn't want to think about his feelings for Grace and the girls. He still had no intention of offering her anything that looked like a future. He just wanted to get to her now, to let her know what he suspected.

The drive to Wichita seemed to take forever. He tried to call her several more times with the same results, but the calls went directly to her voice mail.

Why wasn't she answering the phone? Surely she'd know that so many calls from him would mean he was trying to get in touch with her for an important reason. If she worried about driving and talking, she could always pull to the side of the road to find out what he wanted.

Maybe she doesn't want to talk to you, a little voice whispered in his head. They'd had a beautiful time together; but ultimately he'd never been the brother she'd come for, the one she'd wanted, needed in her life.

When she'd driven away from the ranch, maybe the last thing she'd wanted was to think about or talk to any of the Johnson men again. He couldn't really blame her for that.

But he had to talk to her whether she wanted to hear from him or not. She needed to know his suspicions. The more he thought about it, the more it made sense. He'd be a fool not to consider that the person who stood to gain the most if anything happened to her was her sister.

Grace had told him that the children had gotten the bulk of whatever estate her mother had possessed. If anything happened to Grace, the triplets would go to Justin, who could easily be talked out of taking guardianship by a loving, caring aunt. It was what made the most sense and yet what he didn't want to believe.

How on earth was he supposed to talk to Grace about the fact that her sister might not have her best interests at heart when his own brother had been the one who had broken her heart?

As he entered the city limits of Wichita, he figured he'd cross that bridge when he came to it. Right now all he really wanted was to see her and the girls safe and sound and warn her that the danger might be closer than she thought.

Jake had been to Wichita several times in the past, but he didn't really know the city well. He had to stop at a convenience store and ask for directions to Grace's area of town.

When he found her street, some of the adrenaline that had been with him since he'd jumped into his truck finally began to ease somewhat. Within minutes he'd see that she and the girls were fine and the worst that would happen was that he'd feel like more than a bit of a fool for making the race instead of just waiting to contact her by phone.

At least he'd know he'd forewarned her that the danger to her might not be over just because she'd returned to Wichita. She needed to be aware that there could still be trouble here.

He found her address and parked along the curb. It was a neat ranch house painted a soft beige and with darker brown trim. A large oak tree stood in the center of the yard and would provide welcome shade in the summer.

It was obviously a working-class neighborhood, and he imagined that most of the houses were empty at this time of the day, parents working and kids at babysitters or enjoying summer camp.

It was a good place to raise three children, he told himself. The house appeared solid; the neighborhood looked nice. There was no reason why she and the girls couldn't live a happy life right here.

She'd probably been telling the truth when she said she didn't need anything financially from Justin. She'd just wanted a father for her girls.

He got out of the truck and stretched, mentally preparing himself for seeing her again, for guarding his heart against the tug it felt in her direction.

He was here to give her information and nothing more. Nothing had changed as far as he was concerned, and in any case he'd never be the man she truly wanted in her life.

He walked up to the front door and glanced at his watch. It was nap time for the girls, so he decided not to ring the bell or knock on the door.

The front door was glass, and hopefully he could catch her attention by looking through without having to knock and possibly wake the girls.

He peered into the window and for a moment didn't see anyone. Again he wondered if this whole frantic drive to Wichita and his own crazy thoughts about danger everywhere were just long-term moments of total insanity.

Grace insanity. That's what he should call it, the insane desire to see her just one last time, to assure himself that she was really in the right kind of physical condition to take care of herself, of the girls. Or just because he hadn't been ready to tell her goodbye.

He had just about talked himself into turning around and leaving without saying anything to her when he saw the shadow of somebody too tall to be her, tall like a man, inside the house. Whoever it was stood in the hallway to the living room and obviously wasn't aware of Jake's presence at the door.

Who was he? And what was he doing in Grace's house? He mentally shook himself. It was really none of his business. He had no right to know.

As Jake watched, the man turned halfway and Jake saw that he had a gun in his hand. Instantly Jake slammed himself against the side of the house, where he couldn't be seen if the man looked out the front door.

Jake's heart banged hard against his ribs.

He had no idea who the man was in Grace's living room. He definitely had no idea why the man had a gun, but he knew with a certainty that it didn't bode well for Grace. He'd been right. She was in trouble and he knew that if he didn't do something fast and drastic, then disaster was about to strike.

"For God's sake, Natalie, think about what you're doing," Grace pled with her sister. Grace was seated in a chair they'd dragged from the kitchen into the living room, her arms tied to the rungs of the chair back behind her.

Jimmy still held the gun trained on Grace while Natalie began unplugging the flat-screen television and the computer. "Don't forget the jewelry," he said to Natalie. "Thieves would take everything like that they could fence or pawn."

"Got it," Natalie replied.

"Natalie, don't listen to him. Look at me—I'm your sister." Grace had worried about what kind of a man her sister had hooked up with and now she knew—Natalie had hooked up with a dopehead criminal, one who had apparently filled her head with all kinds of bad things.

"You're the reason she didn't get what she deserved," Jimmy replied.

"Shut up," Grace exclaimed. "I wasn't talking to you, I was talking to my sister."

Natalie closed the laptop and whirled to glare at Grace. "That's all you do, Grace. Talk, talk, talk! I'm sick of it. I'm sick of you. Half of the money that went to the triplets was supposed to be mine."

"I'll give you the money," Grace replied hysterically. "Take me to the bank right now and I'll take it out and put it in your hands. You can have all of it. I don't care about it."

"Yeah, right, and then you call the cops and have us arrested," Jimmy said with a sneer. "It's too late for that, Grace. You're a liability."

"Yeah, a liability," Natalie parroted. "Okay," she said to Jimmy. "You can start carrying this stuff out the back door and loading it in the truck."

He walked over to Natalie and gave her a rough kiss on the lips. Grace wanted to gag as she saw the way her sister responded to him, with eager desperation.

But when Jimmy handed Natalie the gun and then picked up the flat-screen television, the first stir of hope filled Grace. If Jimmy walked out with the television, then that would leave her alone with Natalie. Surely if the two sisters were all alone Grace could talk Natalie away from the edge.

"Remember, baby, we're doing this for us, for our future," Jimmy said, and then he walked through the living room and into the kitchen.

Grace waited until she heard the back door open and close and then she gazed at her sister. "Natalie, untie me and let me go." She kept her voice soft and soothing. Natalie's gaze shot all around the room, everywhere but at Grace's eyes.

"Natalie, honey. Untie me and give me the gun," Grace continued. "We'll make this all right. Nothing bad will happen to you, but you have to stop and think. You don't want to do anything now that can't be made right."

"We're making it right. Jimmy and me, we're making it the way it was supposed to be," Natalie replied. "For me. I deserve this." When she finally met Grace's gaze her eyes were still wild and crazy looking. "You made a stupid mistake and Mom gave you almost all the money. I make stupid mistakes and all I get are lectures from you."

"I won't lecture you anymore. I'll let you live your life however you want. Natalie, I love you. I'm your sister. I know you really don't want to hurt me. It's the drugs and Jimmy making you do all this."

Natalie's eyes narrowed and she laughed. "Do you really think this was all Jimmy's idea? He's too stupid to come up with this. This is what *I* want, Grace. I want you gone from my life forever. Don't worry, I'll see that your brats are fed and clothed, but from here on out I call the shots. I'll have the money to do whatever I please and won't have to answer to anyone, especially you!"

It was at that moment that any hope Grace might have had died and one of her "brats" woke up and began to cry.

Chapter 12

The first thing Jake did was call 911 on his cell phone and give them Grace's address. He had no idea if the dispatcher took him seriously, had no idea how long it might take for the cops to arrive. He only knew he couldn't cool his heels and do nothing.

But what could he do? He was unarmed and unaware of Grace's or the babies' whereabouts in the house. He couldn't ride to the rescue when he wasn't sure exactly what was taking place inside. The last thing he wanted to do was bust inside and cause more danger.

The only thing he knew for sure was that a man brandishing a gun shouldn't be inside Grace's house. The only thing he knew for certain was that he had a sick, urgent feeling inside his very soul.

It was at that moment he remembered the gun in his glove box, the gun he'd placed there for safekeeping on the night he'd taken Grace to the hospital. He'd forgotten about it and apparently so had she when she'd packed up and left Cameron Creek earlier that day.

Jake made his way back to his truck and breathed a sigh of relief as he plucked the gun from inside the glove box. It was a nine-millimeter and fit comfortably in his hand. It took him only a moment to check to make sure it was loaded and ready to go.

Now that he was armed, he intended to get a better look inside to see if he could discern exactly where Grace and the children were located and get an idea of exactly what in the hell was going on.

He walked stealthily around to the side of the house and peered into the first window he came to. It was obviously the triplets' bedroom, all pink and white and frills.

If he hadn't known anything was wrong in the house by then, he would know it now. All three of the girls were awake and crying to get out of their beds. From where he stood he could see the tears trickling down their cheeks, letting him know they had been crying for several minutes. He could hear their plaintive wails through the glass, piercing straight through his heart.

Grace would have never allowed that to

happen. She was usually there the minute the first of the three woke up from a nap. The knot that was in his chest twisted harder, tighter.

He was about to slide around to the back of the house when he heard the back door open. He peeked around the corner and watched as the tall, thin man he'd seen earlier carried out a computer.

Confusion battled with fear inside Jake. Was there a robbery taking place? An armed robbery or some sort of home invasion? Was Grace unconscious?

Already dead?

The thought nearly crashed him to his knees in agony. He could scarcely breathe as he imagined her hurt or worse. The girls. He had to get inside and save the girls even if it might be too late for Grace.

He couldn't go in through the front door, not knowing exactly what was happening, and it was obvious he couldn't go through the back. But there was no way he intended to stand around and wait for the authorities to arrive.

There was really only one way inside and that was the window to the triplets' room. He used his car key to tear the screen and easily removed it, then used the butt of the gun to break the window just above the lock, hoping the cries of the girls would mask the sound of the breaking glass.

He was aware that at any minute somebody could come into the room to tend to the crying babies, that he could be shot half in and half out of the window itself. But it was obvious the kids had been crying for a little while now and nobody had come to their aid.

That fact only made Jake's heart tighten more in his chest.

He eased in through the window and hit the floor on the balls of his feet. "Da-da?" Bonnie sniffled and held out her arms to him and then the other two did the same.

Their outstretched arms and smiles of relief at the sight of him were nearly his undoing. He wanted nothing more than to pick them all up in his arms and hold them tight, soothe their tears and let them know they were safe. But he couldn't do that until he knew where Grace was and exactly what was going on.

His heart felt as if it bled as he walked past the three cribs and tried to ignore the cries of the little girls. With his heart pounding loudly in his ears, he held the gun tight in his hand and peered out of the room and down the hallway.

Nobody was in sight but he heard Grace's voice coming from the living room. "Natalie, please, let me go. Can't you hear the girls? They're frightened and they're crying. They need me."

"They don't need you. Nobody needs you!" a female voice cried, a voice Jake assumed was Natalie's.

He slid his way down the hallway, checking each room as he went to make sure he didn't run into the man he'd seen earlier. All he knew was the sweet relief that at least for now Grace was well enough to talk, well enough to plead with her sister.

He didn't try to make sense of what was happening, he only knew he wanted it to stop. He didn't want to confront Natalie without knowing where the man he assumed was her boyfriend was…the boyfriend with the gun.

And where were the cops? It felt as if it had been hours since Jake had made that 911 call, although in reality he knew it had only been minutes.

"All done," a deep male voice said. "Everything is loaded up in the truck and we're ready to rock and roll."

Every muscle in Jake's body tightened. He now knew they were all there in the living room. If he was going to make a move it needed to be now, before anyone "rock and rolled."

He just prayed that he was about to do the right thing and that it wouldn't get anyone hurt or killed, especially Grace. He slid a glance around the corner into the living room and what he saw made his heart skip a beat.

Grace was tied to a chair in the middle of the room. Thankfully, she didn't look hurt;

but Natalie and her boyfriend stood in front of Grace and the boyfriend once again had the gun in his hand.

"So, what happens now?" Grace asked. "Do you shoot me right here? Is that what you want him to do, Natalie?"

"I didn't want any of this," Natalie replied. "This is all Mother's fault. If she'd just left her money to me instead of to the triplets then none of this would be happening. It's her fault, and it's your fault for having those kids in the first place."

"If you allow this to happen, then it's nobody's fault but your own, Natalie," Grace replied, and Jake heard the weary resignation in her voice.

"Let's get this done," Jimmy exclaimed. "We've been here too long as it is."

Jake knew he could wait no longer. He

whirled into the living room, his gun pointed directly at Jimmy's chest. Thankfully Jimmy's hand with the gun was at his side. He'd obviously not expected anyone else in the house.

"Either one of you twitch and you're dead," Jake said, his gaze focused on the biggest threat—Jimmy and the gun.

"What the hell?" Jimmy exclaimed, but he didn't move. He must have believed the cold resolve Jake knew was in his own eyes. He'd shoot the kid without his heart skipping a beat to save Grace.

Natalie fell to her knees and began to sob, and at that moment there was a sharp knock on the front door. "Wichita Police Department," a deep voice yelled.

"In here," Jake cried out.

Two uniformed policemen entered the room

and immediately took control of the situation. Jake was disarmed and handcuffed along with Jimmy and Natalie, and then Grace was untied from the chair.

To everyone's surprise except Jake's, she ran out of the room and down the hallway. One of the officers ran after her while the other kept his gun trained on the three adults left cuffed and standing in the living room.

Jake knew she'd go to her girls, all of whom had been crying since Jake had entered the house. He couldn't imagine what it had been like for her, to be tied to a chair not knowing if she was going to live or die while her babies cried for her from another room.

Although Jake was handcuffed, he wasn't worried. He knew the officers had cuffed him for their own protection, because they'd walked into a situation they didn't understand

and because Jake had been one of the men with a gun. He knew that once Grace had a minute to talk to the officers he'd be freed and everything would be sorted out.

Natalie hadn't stopped crying since he'd appeared on the scene and she'd realized the scheme had been foiled and they'd been caught. Jimmy looked sullen and scared. He should be scared. He and Natalie would be looking at attempted murder charges.

Grace came back into the room carrying Casey, and the officer followed behind her with Bonnie and Abby in his arms. "He's a good guy," Grace said and pointed a finger at Jake.

"I'm the one who called you guys," Jake said.

"If you'll release him then he can help me put up a playpen for the girls," she said. Jake noticed she didn't spare a glance for her sister or Jimmy.

The officer released Jake from his cuffs and together he and Grace set up a playpen that had been folded up and hidden behind the sofa.

Within minutes the three girls were in the playpen and the officers were asking for answers. "They were going to kill me," Grace said to the man who'd identified himself as Officer Jacobs, and who appeared to be in charge. "They were going to make it look as if I disturbed a robbery and then they were going to shoot me." Only the faint tremble in her voice gave away how distraught she was as she sank down on the sofa.

"He made me do it," Natalie exclaimed, tears cascading down her cheeks. "It was all Jimmy's idea and he beats on me all the time and I was so afraid not to do what he told me to do." She tried to step closer to Grace, but the other officer, Officer James, jerked her back. "Grace, tell them…tell them I'm not really a part of this, that it's not what it looks like. Tell them to let me go, that I'm innocent."

Jake felt Grace's pain as she looked at her sister. He knew exactly what she was thinking, what she was feeling; but he was afraid of what she might say, what she might do.

Would she save her sister, as he'd saved his brother so many times in the past? Would she be in a sense of denial about what had happened here today? About what part Natalie might have played in it?

"I love you, Natalie." The words caused pain to cross Grace's features. "But I can't save you. What you tried to do here is beyond belief. You need help and you need to stay as far away from me and my girls as possible."

"We need to get everyone down to the police station and sort all this out," Officer Jacobs said. By this time three more patrol cars had arrived. Jimmy was loaded in one and Natalie in a second. Grace and the girls went into the third car and Jake found himself alone in the back of Officer Jacobs and Officer James's car.

He'd seen the questions in Grace's eyes as she'd gotten into the police car and knew she was wondering what had brought him back here. He'd also seen her gratitude and knew she was wondering how he'd managed to be here in time to save her life.

He'd seen something else in the depths of her eyes when her gaze had lingered on him—a hint of hope. And that scared him almost as much as whirling around the corner of the living room to confront Jimmy and Natalie.

Was she entertaining some kind of hope that he'd come back here for her and the girls? Hope that he'd shown up here to offer her a future with him? Could she believe that he was here to give her the happily-ever-after she wanted?

She'd just had the biggest betrayal of her life by her sister, coming on the heels of the biggest disappointment in her life from Justin. He hated that it was possible he was going to be the third blow to her world that would send it all completely crashing apart.

Afternoon turned into evening as the questions continued. The triplets had eaten a dinner brought in by a female cop around five. They'd sat on a blanket on the floor in one of the conference rooms and had eaten French fries and grapes, a few chunks of apple and crackers. Not exactly the best meal, but adequate enough to fill their bellies while the adults worked on the details of the crime.

Grace felt as if her heart would never truly heal from Natalie's actions. No matter what happiness she found in her future, there would always be a tiny scar left behind by Natalie.

Still, as she told the police what had happened, what Natalie and Jimmy had planned and why, there was also a part of her heart that hardened where her sister was concerned.

Natalie had crossed a line Grace had never even seen coming. Grace had made excuses for Natalie's selfishness in the past, she'd overlooked a meanness of spirit that her sister possessed, but now she recognized the depth of malevolence Natalie had. Grace knew her sister belonged in prison along with her boy-friend, Jimmy.

Throughout the questioning process Grace tried to keep thoughts of Jake out of her mind, but it was impossible not to wonder why he'd shown up when he had. What had brought him to her when she had needed him most?

If it hadn't been for him she might have been killed. She wanted to believe that when it actually came time for Jimmy to pull the trigger and kill her Natalie would have inter-vened to stop him, but in her heart of hearts she just didn't believe that.

Jake had saved her life. He'd allowed her to live to continue to raise her daughters. But what had brought him to Wichita in the first place?

She wanted to believe it was love. Love for her and her daughters, his need to be with them forever and always.

She wanted that. She wanted it so much it ached inside her as much as her shoulder ached from the renewed insult of having her arm jerked up behind her and tied to a chair.

But she was afraid to embrace that hope. With everything that had gone so crazy since she'd arrived back home, she was afraid to even wish for a little bit of happiness and love.

It was after nine by the time she finished up with the police. The girls had fallen asleep on the blanket and Grace felt as if she'd been in the midst of a tornado that had finally stopped blowing destructive winds.

"I'll have Officer James take you home," Sergeant Walker said when the questioning was finally over. "We'll hold your sister and Jimmy overnight and they'll be arraigned first thing in the morning on attempted murder charges."

"What about Jake Johnson? Is he still here?" she asked.

Sergeant Walker shook his head. "We let him go about an hour ago. You were lucky he realized you might be in trouble from somebody close to you here in town and followed you back here."

So that's what had brought him here, she thought. It hadn't been the need to tell her he wanted her forever and always. He'd somehow figured out that the danger to her was here rather than from some source in Cameron Creek and he'd come to warn her. He'd tried to get her on the phone and when she hadn't answered he'd jumped in his truck and had driven here.

There was no question in her mind that he'd come to care deeply about her and the girls, but he was probably halfway back to his ranch by now, back to living the life he wanted—a life alone.

If was Officers James and Jacobs who helped carry the sleeping babies to the patrol car that had been equipped with three child seats in the back.

As she watched the officers carefully buckling her daughters into the seats, tears sprang to her eyes as she realized how very close she had come to being lost to them.

She wished she had six arms so she could wrap each of them in a set and hold them close for at least the next twenty-four hours.

On the drive back to her house she thought

of how easily she'd been able to give Jake advice about Justin, never seeing the depth of her own issues with Natalie. She owed Jake an apology. Heck, she even owed Justin and Shirley one for believing that they might have been behind the attacks on her.

"You okay?" Officer James asked softly.

She flashed him a forced smile. "As well as I can be considering my sister and her boyfriend had plans to kill me."

"Is there anyone you'd like me to call for you? Maybe somebody to come over and stay for the rest of the night with you?"

"No, thanks. I'll be fine." She appreciated the man's concern, but the danger was over now and she would be fine alone. She had spent most of her life being fine alone. She was just tired, more of an emotional weariness than a physical one.

She'd scarcely had time to process leaving Jake before she'd been thrust into a life-or-death situation. She was truly alone now. No father for her babies, no sister to deal with and no Jake to love.

She even lacked in the friend department. The few single women she'd run around with before she'd gotten pregnant had drifted away after the triplets were born. Grace understood. They were at a place in their lives that didn't include diapers and drooling multiplied by three, and Grace didn't have the time or energy to feed a friendship the way it should be fed.

"I'll help you unload the kids," Officer James said as he pulled up in her driveway.

"Thanks, I appreciate it." She opened the passenger door and stepped out into the darkness of the night. As she opened one back door, Officer James opened the other.

"I can take it from here," a familiar deep voice said.

Grace straightened and looked across the top of the car to see Jake. She couldn't help the way her heart leapt in response. She reached into the backseat and unbuckled Bonnie, then pulled the little one into her arms.

By the time she reached the other side of the car Jake had both Abby and Casey in his arms. The girls were all asleep and remained so as she and Jake walked inside and put them down in their cribs.

Grace had a million questions for him. Why was he still here? What had made him realize the danger was here? And why was he still here? If he'd only come back to warn her, to save her, then why hadn't he just driven back home after he'd left the police station?

She started out of the room, but paused and watched as he moved a tall dresser over in front of the window. She frowned at him in curiosity as they left the room together.

"I broke that window to get inside earlier," he explained. "The dresser will have to stay there until it's fixed."

"I'll have it fixed tomorrow," she replied. They entered the living room and she motioned him to the sofa, trying not to feel anything when she looked at him, wishing she had the numbness of shock to insulate her against her love for him.

"It seems as though I'm always thanking you for something. Tonight I'm thanking you for my life. How did you know?"

"I didn't know for sure. I just started wondering if maybe that car accident you'd been in before coming to Cameron Creek had been intentional, and that meant whoever was trying to hurt you was from here." As always, his eyes were dark and unreadable. "It suddenly seemed important to me that I tell you, and when I couldn't get you on your phone I jumped in the truck and drove here."

"Thank God you did." She leaned back against the sofa cushion and shook her head. "I had no idea the depths of Natalie's hatred for me. I always just wanted what was best for her. I wanted her to be happy."

"I have a feeling all the money in the world won't make Natalie happy. She has issues that even wealth can't solve," he said softly.

"I know. And I'm sorry I suspected your brother and Shirley."

He gave her a wry grin. "Hell, I suspected them for a little while. No apology necessary."

"So, I guess that's it. Mystery solved and life goes on." She told herself the burn at her eyes had nothing to do with telling him good-bye yet again, but rather because of a culmination of everything that had happened since she'd arrived home. Her heart felt too big for her chest as she looked at him. "You should probably head home. You have a long drive ahead of you."

It would be an appropriate thing to do for her to offer him her guest room and suggest he make the drive first thing in the morning. But she didn't think she could stand having him beneath her roof for a single night, and she didn't think she could survive yet another goodbye in the morning.

"You know, I was going to head home

straight from your place once an officer took me back to my truck. I even got on the highway to head home and then turned around and came back."

"You wanted to explain to me why you thought I might be in trouble. I appreciate you stopping by." The words tasted tragic on her lips.

"That wasn't what made me come back. Right after you left earlier this morning, I walked back into the house and there was blessed silence." He got up from the sofa and paced across the floor in front of her, as if too agitated to sit still.

"It was the kind of silence I'd dreamed about, the kind I'd sworn I wanted for the rest of my life." He stopped and stared at her. "And I hated it. You were right, you know. I've spent most of my time taking care of

Justin and had decided to spend the rest of my life running away from my own."

A tiny ray of hope sparked in her heart, but she was afraid to fan it in any way, afraid to allow it to burst into full flame. For all she knew he was just telling her he was grateful for her and the girls bringing him to life, a life he intended to live with somebody else.

"When I got here and realized you were in trouble, I looked for a way to get inside and saw the girls crying. I felt their cries deep in my heart, in my soul. And when I broke through that window and stepped into the bedroom, Bonnie smiled through her tears, called me da-da and raised her hands to me."

Grace was riveted to the sofa, afraid she was somehow misunderstanding what he was telling her. She didn't want to be wrong. Despite her need to keep control of her hope, it had grown so big in her heart she felt as if she might suffocate.

"So you've decided you want children," she finally managed to say.

He smiled then, that warm, wonderful smile that shot heat through her. "No, Grace, what I'm saying is that I want your children. I want you and your children. I love you and I love those girls as if they were my own." His smile faltered and failed. "But I'm also aware that I'm not Justin and maybe whatever feelings you have for me are because I look like the man you came for, because I look like the man you want to father your children, their real father."

"Are you crazy? You don't look like Justin at all. You look like Jake, the man I fell in love with, the man I wished was the real father of my babies. I love you, Jake, and I'm not a bit confused between you and Justin."

"If that's true then why are you still sitting on the sofa?" he asked, the smile once again lighting his features. "Why aren't you in my arms?"

She flew off the sofa and into his waiting arms, her heart beating a million miles a minute as he wrapped her in a tight embrace and they shared a kiss that held all her longing, all her dreams, all her love for him.

When the kiss ended he gazed down at her. In the depths of his beautiful midnight-blue eyes she saw her future. "I want to marry you, Grace. I want to be a stepfather to the girls. I want that big ranch house to be filled with love and happiness like it has never known before."

Grace's heart expanded. Justin would always

be the triplets' father, but she knew that Jake would be the man they could depend on, the man they would run to, the man they would call dad.

"MysteryMom got it right after all," she murmured. "She reunited me with the father of my children and gave me the love of my life. Does it get any better than this?"

Jake's eyes shimmered with promise. "Trust me, it gets so much better than this." He kissed her again and Grace knew she'd found her happily-ever-after in Jake's arms.

Epilogue

"Bonnie, don't pull Daddy Jake's hair like that. He'll be bald before he's forty," Grace said.

"Bald." Bonnie nodded and yanked on Jake's hair again. He laughed, kissed her on the cheek and set her on the grass where her sisters were enjoying cookies.

Grace handed Bonnie her cookie and then she and Jake sat in the nearby lawn chairs. It was early September and a perfect evening to enjoy being outside.

It had been a summer of change. Kerri and Jeffrey had moved out of the ranch house and Grace and the girls had moved in. She and Jake had married in a simple ceremony at City Hall in Cameron Creek. Kerri and Jeffrey had been their witnesses, and Justin had been MIA.

Grace had sold her home in Wichita and torn up her teaching contract. For the next couple of years she would be a stay-at-home mom/rancher's wife, and when the girls were old enough to start school she would perhaps return to teaching.

Natalie and Jimmy were still in jail awaiting trial on the attempted murder charges, and although there was still some residual pain in Grace's heart where Natalie was concerned, she spent little time or energy thinking about the sister who had betrayed her.

After the wedding Justin had moved to Texas to work and try to get his life together. He spoke to Jake occasionally, but still showed little interest in being any kind of a presence in the lives of his daughters.

Grace knew there would come a time when she and Jake had a lot of explaining to do to the triplets. But at the moment that time seemed far away, and Grace's life was filled with too much happiness to worry about it.

As Abby got to her feet and started running away from the blanket, Jake turned to Grace. "Your turn," he said with a grin.

Grace got up from her chair and ran after Abby. When she reached the child, she scooped her up in her arms and kissed her cheek. "We're all sitting right now," she said as she plopped Abby back down next to her sisters.

She returned to her chair and Jake reached for her hand. She smiled at him as she saw the heat in his gaze. "You're having naughty thoughts, Daddy Jake."

He grinned. "I am. I'm thinking that after the girls go to bed I'm going to ravish you."

His words created a pool of heat in her very center. "And it will be your last time ravishing me as the girls' stepfather."

"I know." His gaze went from her to the girls and Grace saw his love for them on his face. "It's the first and best unselfish thing Justin has ever done in his life."

Grace squeezed his hand. Justin had signed his parental rights over to Jake, and tomorrow they would go to court for Jake's official adoption of the girls. "Having second thoughts?"

He looked back at her. "No, I can't wait to

make it official. They're already the daughters of my heart. After tomorrow they'll be my daughters by law."

"Have I told you lately how much I love you?" Grace asked.

"Yes, but I never get tired of hearing it," he replied.

"I love you…and it's your turn." She pointed to Casey, who was up and running.

As Jake jumped up and ran after her, his laughter filling the evening air, Grace's heart was at peace. When she'd arrived here at the ranch for the first time she hadn't been sure exactly what she was looking for, but as she watched Jake drop down in the middle of the triplets, she knew she had found it. She had found her soul mate.

* * * * *

Discover Pure Reading Pleasure with

Visit the Mills & Boon website for all the latest in romance

Buy all the latest releases, backlist and eBooks

Find out more about our authors and their books

Join our community and chat to authors and other readers

Free online reads from your favourite authors

Win with our fantastic online competitions

Sign up for our free monthly eNewsletter

Tell us what you think by signing up to our reader panel

Rate and review books with our star system

www.millsandboon.co.uk

 Follow us at twitter.com/millsandboonuk

 Become a fan at facebook.com/romancehq